In Pursuit of the Truth

Danger in Destiny
Book 6

Melanie D. Snitker

DALLIOU MEDIA, LLC

In Pursuit of the Truth
Danger in Destiny: Book 6
By Melanie D. Snitker

All rights reserved
© 2024 Melanie D. Snitker

Dallionz Media, LLC
P.O. Box 5283
Abilene, TX 79608

Cover Art: Dallionz Media, LLC

For permission requests, please contact the author at the email below or through her website.

Melanie D. Snitker
melanie@melaniedsnitker.com
www.melaniedsnitker.com

*In memory of our
German shepherd, Natty.
We love and miss you!*

Chapter One

Bailey Thompson scooped up her dark blonde hair and twisted it into a messy bun. She glanced at her reflection in the mirror and frowned. One of these days, she was going to get her hair cut and styled. Maybe dye it something bold. A shade of blue would pair nicely with her gray-blue eyes.

She gave herself a scowl. Who was she kidding? Not only didn't she have time for silly things like lengthy hair salon appointments, but she wasn't sure she even had the energy. Not with a farm and two little boys to take care of.

As though Seth had been reading her thoughts, the five-year-old boy shouted from the other end of the house. "Mom! Something's wrong with Poppy!"

Poppy was one of three miniature goats they kept on Thompson Family Farms. Visitors loved the animals' cute bleats and funny antics. Her boys, Seth and three-year-old Jordan, treated the goats like puppies.

The problem was that Poppy shouldn't be within eyesight of the house. Normally, the goats were kept secure in their pen by the small barn, especially overnight.

Her reflection and hair forgotten, Bailey dashed through the house to the front room where Seth was standing on the couch, his arms resting against the back as he looked out the large window. Jordan was copying his brother. Even though he was two years younger, he wasn't much smaller than his big brother thanks to genetics from her dad's side of the family.

Seth looked over his shoulder, saw his mom, and pointed. "See? I think she's hurt!"

Bailey barely had time to spot the animal's form before Seth jumped off the couch and raced for the front door.

"Stop!" Bailey's firm voice had its intended effect.

Seth turned to look at her, his eyes wide.

She pointed to the couch. "I want you and Jordan to stay on the couch. I'm going to check on Poppy, and then I'll be back. Don't leave this house. Do you understand?"

"Yes, ma'am." Seth plopped down on the couch next to his brother.

Jordan nodded emphatically. "Yes, ma'am."

His little voice would have brought a smile to Bailey's face if she hadn't been so focused on the reason why Poppy might be running around the farm. She and the boys always took a quick drive around the property in her pickup truck after dinner to check on the animals and make sure the main gates leading onto the farm were closed and locked. Everything had checked out last night, and all animals were where they should have been.

She shoved her worry down and gave her sons what she hoped was a reassuring smile. "I'll be right back. You can watch me from the window."

With that, she stepped outside, closed the door behind her, and hurried toward the goat's form. To her relief, Poppy lifted her head and gave a sad bleat. At least the animal was still alive.

"What happened, Poppy Girl? What did you get yourself into?"

Bailey knelt beside Poppy, who struggled to her feet. A gash ran several inches down one of her legs, and her hoof was stained with blood. Bailey ran her hands over the animal's body, checking for any other injuries. When none were present, she gave a sigh of relief. She'd need to take Poppy to the livestock vet they used and have the gash stitched up and wrapped, but it could've been so much worse.

Still, none of this explained how the goat got out of her pen in the first place or how she was hurt.

Thankfully, it was Thursday, and the farm was closed to the public until tomorrow. At least Bailey wouldn't be rushing to get everything cleaned up before visitors came by. On the other hand, if Rachel, the country store manager, were coming in today, then Bailey would have some extra help.

She'd considered expanding their small petting zoo beyond the goats and ducks they already had. Now, she was glad they hadn't. Sometimes the three goats and six ducks were more than she could handle.

Bailey ran a comforting hand over the goat's white and brown head. "We're going to take good care of you. But first, we need to check on your sisters." With a grunt, she scooped the goat into her arms and carried her to the front of the house. "Seth! Come on out here, please."

The words had barely left her mouth when the front door flew open. Seth ran onto the porch, followed by Jordan.

"What happened to her, Mom? Is she going to be okay?"

Jordan stood, his thumb in his mouth, and stared with wide eyes at the injured leg.

"She'll be fine. We need to take her to the vet, but first, we have to check on the other goats. I want you to sit right here and hold Poppy while I get a few things." She set the goat down, made sure that Seth had a tight hold on her, and then picked up Jordan. "I'll be right back."

Five minutes later, both boys had their shoes on, and she had her pistol in its holster, concealed in the waist of her jeans. She helped them into the old pickup truck she used around the farm. Once they were both secure in their booster seats, she heaved Poppy inside and set her on a blanket at Seth's feet.

Bailey followed the gravel road that led from the front of their house, around a small peach orchard, and toward the red barn. The goat pen was set up along one side of the barn on the outside.

Along the way, she kept her eyes open for the other two goats in case they'd all somehow managed to get out.

She sought out the goat pen, and her stomach sank when she saw that it was empty.

"Mom? Where are Pansy and Petunia?" There was no missing the worry in her oldest son's voice.

"I'm not sure. Stay in the truck. I'm going to take a closer look at the gate. I'll be right back."

Bailey didn't wait for his response. She turned off the engine and climbed out of the truck. The gate hadn't just come open. It'd been destroyed. Pieces of wood littered the ground in front of the pen.

She ran a finger over the smooth ends of the wood.

Someone had gone so far as to cut through the wood with a saw or something similar.

Her gaze caught on the blood that stained one of the more jagged spots low on the gate.

Bailey imagined Poppy cutting her leg on it as she squeezed through the hole. The goats were curious, but she couldn't imagine Poppy forcing her body through hard enough to cause that much damage. Not unless she'd been scared. Had something—or someone—chased them out of their pen?

Where were the other two goats?

The hair stood up on the back of her neck, and a chill ran up her spine. She scanned the area, shading her face with her hand as she peered toward the east. Nothing else seemed out of place, but she couldn't shake the feeling that someone was watching her.

She needed to check on the ducks and then make sure the rest of the property was okay. What if the goat pen wasn't the only thing that had been vandalized?

Her heart twisted, and she fought to keep an echoing grimace from her face.

All of this would've been easier if Joe were here. He'd take care of everything—fixing the fence, checking the property, and ensuring their family was safe.

It'd been over two years since a car accident took her husband's life and changed everything. Two years since she'd started managing all of this with the help of some friends who refused to let her retreat when things got hard.

That was especially true of Nate Walker, who'd been their friend even before she and Joe married. Nate and Joe had met while working for the Destiny Police Department. He was just one of several other officers at the precinct who had become family friends.

Nate took an extended leave of absence early last year after an especially difficult case that he still didn't talk about. Before that, he was a police detective, and an amazing one, according to Joe. Nate always insisted that she call him if she ever needed something.

A sound from the truck drew her attention. Seth had rolled a window down and stuck his head out. "Mom! Poppy's getting blood all over."

Bailey was confident enough to admit she was stubborn and preferred to do things on her own. Today, however, was too much.

She bit the inside of her cheek as she pulled the phone from her back pocket. Before she had a chance to talk herself out of it, she dialed Nate's number.

His deep voice, one she'd recognize anywhere, responded after a single ring. "Hey, Bailey. Are you and the boys okay?"

"We're fine, but we had some trouble." She took in a steadying breath. "I could really use your help."

"I'm on my way. Tell me what's going on."

Chapter Two

Nate flexed his hands around the steering wheel and focused on the road ahead of him. He listened as Bailey told him what happened, her voice tight with unease, and wished he didn't live on the other side of town.

He'd often worried about Bailey and her young sons living in the country alone. They didn't even have a dog on the property to warn them if someone started sneaking around.

Nate thought about his own Rottweiler, Minnie. He'd feel a lot better if Bailey had a dog like that roaming her house and property. In general, Minnie was an absolute teddy bear, but she certainly didn't look it. Sometimes, those first impressions were everything.

Most people—even crooks—had enough common sense to walk away from a place when they saw a large dog protecting it.

He drove his truck across the railroad tracks, the tires bumping over the raised metal rails.

Bailey's voice came over the speaker. "I'm going to take

Poppy into the barn and keep her there until I can get an appointment with the vet."

He shook his head even though she couldn't see it. If the person who had destroyed the goat pen were still in the area, the barn would be the perfect place to hide. "Don't go inside. Stay in the truck with the boys. I'd rather check the barn first and help you get her settled. I'll be there as fast as I can."

There was a moment or two of silence. Nate could imagine the resolute set of her chin and the flash of her blue eyes. She'd instinctively balk at his suggestion because she was always determined to do everything on her own.

He prayed she'd realize just how important it was to keep herself and the boys safe right now. Someone had gone onto her property and intentionally caused damage. There was no reason for that if not to either get attention or work out some anger. Neither set well with Nate.

"Wait seven minutes, Bailey."

"Yeah. Okay. We're in the truck by the barn."

That offered him some relief. Still, he couldn't get there fast enough. "Did you call the police yet?"

"No. You were the first person I thought of."

His heart flip-flopped at her words, and just as he'd done for the last eight years, he ignored the reaction. It didn't matter that he'd fallen for Bailey years ago because even before that it'd been love at first sight between her and Joe, one of his best friends.

It took less than a year for the couple to go from dating to engaged to married.

Nate had wanted nothing more than for the two of them to be happy. Letting anyone know how he felt would've only made everyone uncomfortable and likely ruined the friendships he had with them both. He'd buried the feelings down deep and hoped to eventually meet a woman who could capture his heart like Bailey had.

He was still waiting.

"I'm at the gate now." He'd insisted she stay on the phone until he got there. He rolled the window down and entered the security code on the keypad. The metal gate swung open, and he drove through, pressing the gas pedal and making his way to the barn.

Bailey's old, gray pickup was right where she said it would be. Their phone connection ended as she got out of the truck and closed the door behind her.

Nate noted the stress on her face and the worry flashing in her pretty blue eyes. Then he noticed the blood on her pants.

She looked down and frowned. "It's Poppy's. I was going to put her in the barn until I could get an appointment. I need to drive through the property and make sure nothing else has been damaged."

All while trying to keep two active little boys happy. Speaking of which, they were both waving at him, big smiles on their faces, as they looked out the truck windows. He grinned and waved back, hoping to put them at ease.

He turned his attention to her. "I'll go check out the barn. Call the police and report what happened. Then call the vet and see if you can take Poppy in. Okay?"

Thankfully, she nodded and turned to climb into the truck.

Whoever vandalized the goat pen was likely long gone. Should be, if they had any sense whatsoever. Still, Nate would feel better once he'd cleared the barn.

He opened the doors wide, reassured by the weight of his handgun tucked into the holster inside the waist of his pants.

The barn was only a few years old. There were three stalls and a large storage area for hay, grain, and other feeding supplies. The other side of the barn served as more of a garage for tools, a riding lawn mower, and things like that.

Everything seemed to be in order. Nate went through to reassure himself that no one was hiding.

When he got back to the truck, Bailey was leaning against the closed door, her phone to her ear. Her gaze swung to meet his. "All right, thank you. I'll bring her right in." She hung up and slipped the phone in her back pocket. "They said I can go ahead and bring Poppy in first thing." She cut a glance at the back door of her truck.

"Did you call the police?"

Bailey nodded. "Jenny is on her way out."

"Good." Officer Jenny Durant had also worked with both Nate and Joe at the precinct. "As soon as she arrives, I'll take Poppy to the vet for you. That way you can be here to answer any of Jenny's questions. I'll take Jordan with me."

One of Bailey's eyebrows lifted. "You sure about that?"

Nate might have chuckled in a different situation. There was no doubt the youngest boy was full of energy and could be a bit of a handful, which is exactly why Nate wanted to take him along. "Yep. Seth can help you clean things up if needed and get the rest of the chores done."

"Thanks, Nate." One corner of her mouth pulled to the side. She slipped her hands into her pockets and leaned back against the truck. "I don't understand why anyone would do this. Was there any sign of someone breaking through the main gate?"

"It was secure when I arrived." Although with 400 acres, someone could have gone over the fence at any other point. The fences around here were to mark the property lines, but they didn't do much to deter someone from crossing them if they chose to do so. He didn't voice his thoughts, though. Chances were, Bailey had already considered it. If she hadn't, there was no need to bring that fear to mind right now. "Let me grab the crate and put it in the back of my truck for Poppy."

As sympathetic as he was toward the poor goat, he didn't want to get blood in the cab of his truck. Plus, a loose animal in the back with Jordan while on the road was a recipe for disaster.

Bailey gave him a nod. "Thanks again." With that, she went back to her vehicle to check on the boys.

Nate found the kennel in the barn, loaded it into the back of his truck, then secured it in place with rope. By the time he'd finished, a police car was driving toward them. Bailey must have given Jenny the code to the gate.

He jumped down from the bed of his truck just in time to watch Jenny give Bailey a hug before waving at him.

"Hey, Nate."

"Good to see you, Jenny. Thanks for coming so quickly."

"Of course." Jenny smiled, but there was a shadow of concern on her face.

They'd spoken after Joe's funeral and had agreed that, between the two of them, they'd make sure Bailey had any help she needed. Of course, the stubborn woman liked to do things on her own, but it didn't stop them from trying.

The fact that someone had come onto Bailey's property and caused damage at all was a problem.

Jenny motioned toward the goat pen. "I'm going to go take a quick look and snap a few pictures."

Bailey tilted her head toward her truck. "Sounds good. I'll get Jordan's booster seat out."

Nate followed Jenny to the pen. There was no doubt that someone had intentionally cut the wood.

"It was premeditated." His voice came out as more of a growl than he'd intended. He glanced at Bailey's truck and lowered his voice. "If someone had just wandered onto the property and decided to destroy something, boards would be broken, not cut."

Jenny took several photos with her phone. "But why the goat pen? Was anything else damaged?"

"Not that Bailey noticed, but she said she still needed to drive around and check out everything else. You'll go with her for that?"

He'd rather take on the job himself, but he also wanted to ease some of the burden from Bailey's shoulders by taking Poppy to the vet.

"Of course. I won't leave until you get back." She gave him a contemplative look. "We really could use you back at the department. You've always had an eye for the details."

"I appreciate that." But he wasn't ready. He didn't need to speak the words aloud, though. Jenny knew what had prompted his extended leave of absence from his job as police detective, and she wouldn't push.

He truly appreciated knowing that his friends and co-workers wanted him back.

"If you and Bailey find anything else, let me know."

"Will do." Jenny turned back to the pen.

Nate jogged over to Bailey's truck and lifted the booster seat from her arms. "I've got it." He put it in the center of the back seat of his own vehicle and secured it in place.

Next, he opened her truck's back door again and

greeted the boys with a smile. "Hey, kiddos. You being good for your mom?"

Jordan nodded his head emphatically while Seth gave Nate a serious look over the top of the small goat he was holding. "Yes, sir."

"Good man. Here, let me take Poppy. Jordan and I are going to take her to the vet. I want you to help your mom while I'm gone."

There was no missing the flash of worry in Seth's eyes as he momentarily tightened his hold on Poppy's neck. But he straightened his spine and leaned back. "Yes, sir. I will."

Nate ruffled his hair before lifting the goat into his arms. By the time he got her in the pen and Jordan transferred to his booster seat and strapped in, the sun was already warming the air.

He turned to find Bailey standing nearby. Her hair, which she'd pulled up in a bun, was coming loose. Several tendrils hung next to her face by one ear. He couldn't remember the last time he'd seen her with her hair down. Maybe a handful of times since Joe died.

"I'll be back as soon as I can."

"Thanks again. The vet has my credit card on file. I'll call ahead and let her know you're on the way, so there won't be any problems charging everything." She scratched at the back of her neck. "Not the way I wanted to start the morning."

"No joke. I'll text you with updates."

A smidge of her stress evaporated, and Nate was happy he could be the one to do that for her. Reluctantly, he climbed into the truck and started it up. With a last glance in the rearview mirror, he prayed that Bailey and Seth stayed safe and that Jenny could find evidence that might lead to whoever did this.

Chapter Three

Bailey and Seth had driven around the property with Jenny to check everything else and keep an eye out for the missing goats. There'd been no sign of them. Bailey had encouraged Seth, saying they might turn up on their own when they weren't as scared. It was certainly a possibility. But with coyotes and other animals out there, Bailey worried they wouldn't see Pansy and Petunia again. She kept those thoughts to herself, though.

Now, she was helping Seth haul piece after piece of broken wood and stack them in a pile. He'd been determined to get them all out of the goat pen so it would be easier for them to repair it later. After all, they would need a place for Poppy to stay once she was all better.

He dusted his hands off and sighed heavily. "I hope we find them soon."

"Me, too, kiddo." She gave him a hug and a kiss on the top of his head. "We'll keep praying they turn up."

Seth nodded and wandered over to the stack of wood, where he started to climb on some of the lower pieces.

Jenny, who had been walking through the trees and brush in case the person responsible had ditched the saw they used, came up to stand beside Bailey empty handed. She nudged her friend's shoulder. "You've got a good kid there."

"Sure do. Sometimes, I worry he has too much responsibility."

"Are you kidding?" Jennie brushed some dust off her uniform pants. "You make sure those boys have so much fun. Not to mention, they get to live out here with all this space, interesting pets, and daily adventures. Trust me, he's fine, and you're a great mom."

Bailey prayed that was true.

She and Jenny had been friends since they'd worked together at a local restaurant right after high school, and it was through Jenny that she'd met both Nate and Joe. Bailey remembered the day Jenny had told her she'd decided to become a police officer. Bailey thought she'd been kidding. At first, she couldn't imagine her friend going through the Police Academy and wearing a uniform.

It didn't take long to realize that Jenny had a giving, caring attitude that, in combination with her determination, made her so good at being a cop. It was no wonder Jenny thrived at her job.

Today, Bailey was thankful to have her there not only as an officer but also as a trusted friend.

The rumble of an engine brought their attention to Nate's truck as he guided it down the road to the barn. He caught her gaze and gave her an encouraging smile as he helped Jordan out of the back. The little boy practically jumped from Nate's arms and raced to Bailey.

"Poppy is all fixed!" he announced proudly.

"I'm so glad." Bailey swung him into her arms and gave

him a big hug. He barely hugged her back before he was squirming to get down again.

Seth's bright eyes took in Nate, then swung to his truck. "So Poppy's going to be okay?"

"She'll be fine. The vet had to stitch up her leg and bandage it. She'll be taking some medication to keep away infection. But in ten to fifteen days, she should be as good as new."

"Yay! Thanks, Nate!" With that, Seth ran to the back of the truck and hopped onto the bumper so he could visit with the goat.

Jordan tried to follow suit, but his shorter legs weren't cooperating.

Bailey grinned and shook her head. What was she going to do with the pair of them? Her heart swelled when Seth reached down and pulled his little brother up alongside him.

She was so thankful for their close relationship and prayed it would continue to be that way as they grew up.

Nate gave the boys an approving look before turning his attention to Bailey. "The vet gave us antibiotics. There shouldn't be any permanent damage, although there'll always be a scar. It's best to keep her in the barn until it heals, though. It'll be easier to keep an eye on it." He tilted his head toward the goat pen. "I'll help you rebuild the gate and fence in the next few days."

"I appreciate that. Thank you."

"Of course." His gaze lingered on her for a heartbeat before he addressed Jenny. "Did you guys find anything else?"

"Not a thing." Jenny frowned. "No evidence left behind. No damage was done anywhere else. The whole thing is odd, that's for sure. If it weren't for the saw or ax used, I'd think it was random. When I get back to the station, I'll check the reports for the last couple of weeks and see if anyone else called in something similar."

The temperature was well into the 80s, yet goose bumps rose along Bailey's arms. She scanned the area around them. She'd much rather assume the damage was random and a one-time thing. Just knowing that someone was prowling about her property last night made her incredibly uneasy as well as angry. Seriously, what was wrong with people?

"Let me know if you find anything." Maybe it was a set of restless teens acting on dares. Whoever did this, Bailey hoped Jenny or someone else in the department caught them soon.

"I will. I'd better be getting back. If you have any other trouble, let me know. Okay?" Jenny glanced at the boys. "I'll be praying you find the other two goats."

"Thanks, Jenny." Bailey gave her friend a hug.

"Yep, appreciate it, Durant." Nate gave her a quick hug as well. "Try to stay out of trouble."

"Oh, you know it always has a way of finding me." Jenny grinned. "See you guys later."

Jenny's squad car drove away, leaving a cloud of dust in its wake.

Nate nodded toward his truck. "Let's get Poppy set up, and then I'll take another drive to see if I can spot Pansy and Petunia."

Seth made sure there was plenty of hay in Poppy's new temporary residence. Jordan helped Bailey fill up the water trough while Nate retrieved the goat and carried her into the stable.

The poor thing looked drowsy, and the white bandage

on her leg reminded Bailey how lucky the little goat was to be safe and taken care of.

Regular visitors would miss the chance to pet the goat trio when the farm opened to the public tomorrow and Saturday. She made a mental note to print out flyers asking visitors to keep an eye out for the other two. It certainly couldn't hurt.

Seth was petting Poppy through the slats in the pen. He half-turned. "Mom? Can I help you give her the medicine tomorrow?"

"Of course." Bailey ruffled his hair. "I would really appreciate that."

He nodded and turned his attention back to the goat.

"You boys keep an eye on Poppy. I'll be right back." Bailey motioned for Nate to follow her outside. Once they were out of earshot, she leaned against the edge of the barn. "I really hope we find the other goats. I can't help but worry that, if they wandered far, they may not have survived the night." The thought of the little animals suffering at the teeth of a predator had tears stinging the back of her eyes.

"The possibility occurred to me, too." Nate started to say something else and stopped.

Bailey's eyes narrowed. "What is it?"

"Whoever destroyed the gate might have stolen them, and Poppy was the only one who managed to get away. The goats are small enough. It wouldn't be difficult to lead them to the fence and lift them over."

She wasn't sure which possibility bothered her more. "But if the purpose was to steal the goats, then why destroy the gate in the first place?"

Nate crossed his arms in front of him and shifted his weight from one foot to the other. "We may never know."

He studied her face. "Are you going to be okay here today? Or tonight?"

"I have to be. This is our home. I'm not going to let someone make me feel like I can't stay here." Bailey shrugged, hoping the motion came off as casual.

Nate clearly saw right through her. His arms lowered, and he took a step closer. "Don't hesitate to call me if something else happens."

"We'll be fine."

"I'm serious, Bailey. If you don't call me, then call Jenny."

"Yeah. I will." She was suddenly aware of how close he stood. She looked down at the ground where the toes of their shoes were mere inches apart.

Warmth seeped into her chest and spread straight to her heart. She immediately squelched the response and mentally chided herself.

Ridiculous. Between the stress of the day and wishing that Joe was there with them, it was no wonder her emotions were all over the place.

Nate was an amazing friend who didn't have to step in and help his best friend's wife, but he did it anyway. She and the boys were lucky to have him in their corner.

Chapter Four

What Bailey really needed was a calm afternoon followed by an uneventful evening so she could get a decent night's sleep. Instead, she'd had a difficult time falling asleep, only to be awakened an hour later by a thunderstorm rolling through. There was no tornado activity, but the lightning and thunder were enough to keep her awake. How the boys slept through all that noise, she'd never know.

Once the storm passed, she kept hearing noises outside; her imagination kept playing tricks on her. She'd close her eyes and picture someone sneaking around outside the house. Finally, she checked the windows to make sure they were locked and saw where the rain was dripping onto the windowsill, causing the sounds she'd heard.

It was nearly four in the morning before she finally fell asleep again. The six o'clock alarm sounded way sooner than she was ready for. Two cups of coffee later, and at least she could pretend to feel human again.

"I don't see them anywhere." Seth's voice was laced with disappointment and worry.

Bailey's heart clenched at the sound. They had taken care of Poppy and made sure she was medicated and set for the morning. They'd also fed the ducks and finished their morning chores. Now, they were driving around hoping to spot Pansy and Petunia before opening the country store.

"I don't see them either, sweetie. We might not find them."

"What if a wild animal hurts them?"

Bailey glanced in the rearview mirror to see that Seth's words had brought tears to Jordan's eyes. They'd lost a couple of ducks to coyotes in the past, so the boys weren't unfamiliar with the possibility.

"If they're out there running around, that might happen. But it's also possible that the person who ruined the gate took them. They were so cute. Maybe they sold them to someone else who loves them and is taking care of them."

Another look in the mirror told her Seth wasn't convinced.

"Maybe their new owners are letting them live inside and making them a salad every night for dinner." She hoped the possibility might take some of the sting out. Or at least help the boys focus on something besides the idea that the poor goats were lying somewhere injured or dead.

Seth met her gaze in the mirror. "That person can't love them like we do."

And there it was.

Bailey blinked back the tears that sprang to her eyes. They had a long, busy day ahead of them. She couldn't afford to start crying already.

Thompson Family Farm was only open to the public two days a week, but Fridays and Saturdays were usually packed with people looking for gifts and unique items at the store or one of their homegrown gourds or pumpkins for fall decoration.

One of the biggest draws, however, was the large sunflower field. She and Joe had planted it the year before he died. Everyone loved it, and that included Bailey. There was just something about row after row of bright, cheerful flowers that made her heart feel lighter.

The sunflower field was not only a great place for portraits, but people could pick some for a small fee and take them home if they wanted to.

"All right, let's head to the store. We'll drive around again this evening. Don't forget, we have flyers to hand out. Hopefully, one of the customers will spot them." She wasn't sure how likely that was, but today, they all needed hope and encouragement.

*

Bailey handed a printed receipt to her customer along with a flyer about the missing goats and smiled. "I hope you all have fun. Don't forget to take advantage of our photo wall. Feel free to tag us on social media if you post any pictures."

"We will. Thank you." The customer gave a wave as she corralled her three kids and ushered them out of the little country store. The door had barely closed when someone else came in.

"Sure is busy today." Rachel Carmichael, the store manager, turned to flash a smile.

The woman was in her sixties and had started working for Bailey two years ago. It was such a blessing to have her help because there was no way Bailey could keep up with everything and still watch her sons.

She glanced over at the child-sized table not far away.

Jordan was happily putting a puzzle together. He was content for now, but she knew that would only last so long. There was a small box full of things to play with and do that sat near the table. Hopefully, Jordan would find something else to do when the puzzle no longer held his interest. Meanwhile, Seth was standing at the door and handing shopping baskets to customers as they came in.

Bailey rang up another customer. When there was a break in the crowd, she wiped her hands off on her jeans and turned to Rachel. "Super busy. I think everyone's excited for fall, even if the weather hasn't caught on yet."

It was the middle of September in Destiny, Texas. Temperatures were still in the low nineties most days, but the nights were getting cooler.

The fall produce was ready, and customers seemed excited about the colorful gourds and pumpkins to choose from. In addition to that, the store stocked a variety of Texas-made products, from jams and jellies to toys and candies.

The farm—and its customer base—had grown a great deal since she and Joe first opened it to the public four years ago. This had all been Joe's dream. His hope was to get it established and slowly expand so that, one day, he could retire from the police department, and they could run the farm together every day.

A pang of sadness hit, and Bailey did her best to acknowledge it and then push it back down. It was strange how the grief could punch through at the strangest of times.

Joe would be happy with how the farm was doing but disappointed that it hadn't grown. After losing Joe and managing the boys on her own, Bailey hadn't been up to expanding anything.

She was finally entertaining the possibility. If they

started work in November after the fall season was over, they might be able to open up the new area to the public in the spring. It was a thought, anyway. She was still in the information gathering process for now.

Rachel ran her fingers through her close-cropped gray hair. The older woman had kept the same hairstyle for as long as Bailey had known her.

Rachel always seemed younger than her years, and she related well to the customers. If Bailey was ever able to open the farm to the public more often, would Rachel be willing to work the extra days at that point? She decided to test the waters.

"I've been wondering lately what it would take to bring in enough people to open to the public more than twice a week."

The older woman's brows rose. "Are you finally thinking about expanding? I know you and Joe were considering it, but you haven't mentioned it since..." She gave Bailey a worried look. "I know it hasn't been easy."

Bailey shrugged. No, it hadn't, but life continued to march forward. "I've been thinking about it. Considering the options."

Rachel nodded slowly. "Well, you know I'm happy to help. I love being out here. I'm sure I could work more days into my schedule when the time comes." She smiled sadly. "I only worry about you taking on more than you need to."

"I appreciate that. Thank you."

"Mommy? I'm hungry." Jordan looked up at her, his face serious.

Bailey checked her watch. "I'll get you some lunch in about twenty minutes." She and the boys took the early lunch break. Then Rachel took the later one.

Fridays were busy, but nothing like Saturdays. To help

manage the crowds on Saturdays, Bailey employed several teenagers.

Jordan wrapped his arms around his middle. "But I'm starving!"

"And you'll live for twenty more minutes. Why don't you finish your puzzle and then clean up your crayons? That way, you'll be ready to go when it's time to eat."

The little boy clearly saw through the diversion but refocused on his puzzle anyway.

"Nate!" Seth's excited voice drew Bailey's attention to the door.

Nate had walked into the store, a large bag in one hand. He scooped Seth up with the other. "Hey, kiddo. You helping your mom?"

"Yep. Been handing baskets to customers and cleaning up."

"Good man." Nate set him down and turned to catch Jordan, who had run across the store and thrown himself at him. "Good to see you, too, buddy."

Jordan's arms tightened around Nate's neck, their faces close together. "I'm hungry."

Nate chuckled. "It'll be time for lunch soon." He gave the boy a wink.

With a sigh, Jordan scrambled down and went to pick up his crayons.

Bailey rested her hands on her hips. "I promise I fed them this morning."

Rachel chuckled. "Not to mention all the snacks I've seen them eat." She smiled at Nate. "Good to see you. It's been a while."

"Yeah, it has. I wanted to bring some sandwiches by. I have plenty if you'd like one, Rachel. Turkey and Swiss or ham and cheddar?"

Rachel's eyes brightened at the thought. "You sure you have enough?"

"Absolutely."

Nate set the bag on the counter and was digging through the sandwiches when someone came in through the main door. The man, who looked all business in a pair of slacks and a button-down shirt, took his sunglasses off and tucked them into a pocket on the front of his shirt.

Seth brightened and ran to hand the man a basket but was ignored completely.

Instead, the man took in the store with a critical eye. "I'm looking for Bailey Thompson."

Chapter Five

N ate didn't care for the man immediately, and it wasn't like him to make snap opinions like that about people. Everything about the guy screamed greasy car salesman. It bothered Nate that his first impression was so negative. Then again, he had learned years ago to trust his instincts, and they were telling him that this guy was going to be trouble.

Rachel had asked for a ham and cheddar sandwich. Nate found one, handed it to her, then turned his attention to Bailey as she walked around the counter.

"I'm Bailey Thompson. What brings you to Thompson Family Farm?" She'd put a smile on her face, but it was clearly forced. Good, she'd gotten the same impression.

"Kyle Driver from Driver Real Estate." Instead of shaking her hand or offering a smile of his own, he handed her a business card. "I've got a client who's interested in this property of yours. Four hundred acres, from what I understand. He's willing to offer you a fair price if you'd consider selling it."

By the determined look on his face, Nate guessed Mr.

Driver rarely got turned down. Nate ignored his instinct to walk over and stand beside Bailey. He was there if she needed help. Otherwise, he had no doubt she could handle this.

Bailey glanced at the business card and handed it right back. "Please let your client know that the property is not for sale. I'm sorry you wasted your time coming out."

The realtor's upper lip twitched. "I have the offer right here. I think you might change your mind when you see what kind of numbers we're talking about." He withdrew his phone from a back pocket. "Is there someplace we can discuss this in private?"

Nate didn't miss the way the realtor gave Jordan an annoyed look as though the little boy was smearing feces or climbing the walls instead of cleaning up the small table.

"I don't need to discuss this or see the offer. The property is not for sale. If you'll excuse me, it's time to get my sons some lunch."

Mr. Driver grunted. He plunked the business card down on the counter with a flourish. "Give me a call when you change your mind. But realize that the offer may not be as generous then as it is now."

With that, he turned on his heel and left the store.

Bailey wrinkled her nose. "I feel like I should go behind him with a mop to clean up that trail of slime."

No joke.

"You handled that nicely." Nate gave her an encouraging nod. He reached for the business card. "Mind if I keep it?"

Bailey shrugged.

"This isn't the first time." Rachel chuckled. "She's becoming a pro by now."

His eyes narrowed as he watched Bailey help Jordan

with the last of his crayons. "How often do you get people asking you to sell the place?"

She looked to Seth, who was watching the adults, clearly all ears.

"Let's get the boys some lunch." She reached down and tickled Jordan's stomach. "After all, they might starve to death any minute now." She turned to Rachel. "I'll be back by noon."

"Take your time. I've got lunch right here." She lifted the sandwich and shot Nate a thankful smile.

Fifteen minutes later, the boys were seated at the coffee table in Bailey's living room, their sandwiches and glasses of juice in front of them. A cartoon was playing on the TV, which meant the adults might as well not exist.

Nate accepted a can of soda, which he opened immediately and took a long swig. Bailey sat across from him. He pushed a turkey and Swiss across to her and watched as she unwrapped it and took a bite.

"Are realtors harassing you about selling? How long has that been going on?"

She chewed her bite slowly. There was no doubt she didn't want to talk about it. Nate just wasn't sure if it was the subject in general or if it was him specifically that she didn't want to tell. If it was the latter, it would be hard not to take it personally.

"It started about a year ago." She took a sip of her own soda. "I get one or two requests per week. Most of the time, it's through e-mail or over the phone. But occasionally, a realtor seems to think I'll be more likely to change my mind if they come in person." Bailey shrugged as though it were no big deal. "I can handle it."

"But you shouldn't have to. You shouldn't have to keep telling people that you don't want to sell your farm. To just walk into your place of business today was cold." Nate took a bite out of his own sandwich with more force than was probably necessary. "What I'm wondering is whether there are a bunch of different clients or if there's one particularly determined person who is making their way through realtors hoping you'll eventually say yes. Have they told you why this person wants to buy your place?"

"Not in so many words. Mineral rights have been mentioned. So has using it for residential properties to help Destiny grow, but that was more of a guilt trip. As though it might be my fault if I don't sell and Destiny stagnates." She set her sandwich back down. "I mentioned it to Jenny once, and apparently, they aren't doing anything illegal by asking."

"That's true. But you shouldn't have to deal with this repeatedly." Nate went over the different options, but there really weren't many. Bailey was right; what they were doing might be on the verge of harassment, but they weren't officially doing anything illegal.

"If it *is* just one person or company, I keep hoping they'll eventually give up. Otherwise, maybe the realtors will finally see that approaching me is a complete waste of their time."

Nate finished his sandwich and then leaned his chair onto the back two legs. He studied Bailey. She might be acting calm and collected, but he could tell she was frustrated. "How do you do that?"

Her brows lowered in confusion. "Do what?"

"Take everything in stride."

Her laugh came out like a bark, and she coughed, sobering quickly. "Trust me, I don't. Not internally, anyway." She looked to the doorway that separated the kitchen from the living room. "Sometimes you just do what you have to do."

"You don't always have to do everything on your own."

Her blue eyes widened a little as her gaze met his. "I called you yesterday, didn't I?"

Nate slowly lowered his chair to all four legs. "Yeah, you did."

She'd said he was the first person she'd thought of at the time. That fact meant more to him than it probably should.

He held her gaze. "I want you to promise me you'll call me again if anything else comes up. I don't mind, Bailey. I hope you know that."

A flood of emotions cascaded across her face, but she schooled her expression so quickly it left Nate wondering what it all meant. Instead, she simply nodded her head. Her attention dropped to the remainder of her sandwich, and he barely caught the whispered, "Promise."

Nate truly hoped she would.

In the meantime, he had every intention of checking up on Kyle from Driver Real Estate. If realtors were going to use the land's mineral rights as a reason for Bailey to sell, he wanted to know more about them.

Chapter Six

Bailey and the boys were surprised to find Pansy waiting for them at the barn when they got there the next morning. If Bailey had known how excited the goats would be when they were reunited, she would have taken a video of the reunion. As it was, the goats were standing next to each other as though they were afraid to let each other out of their sight.

Pansy must have either heard or smelled her sister. Other than acting like she was hungry, she didn't look any worse for wear.

Bailey snapped a picture of the duo and sent it to Nate along with a text.

> "Look who showed up this morning out of the blue."

It didn't take long before she received a reply.

> "Wow. I'll bet that was a surprise. Which goat is it?"

"Pansy. Not a scratch on her."

"If only goats could talk."

Bailey chuckled and typed out a response.

"Right? I'd love to know where she's been the last twenty-four hours."

Was Petunia out there somewhere, too? Bailey had just about subscribed to the idea that the goats had been stolen. Maybe they really had run off out of fear, and the only reason Poppy stuck around was because of her hurt leg.

"I'm glad she's okay. I'll bet the boys are relieved."

She took another photo, this one zoomed out to show Seth and Jordan reaching through the fence to pet the goats, and sent it to Nate.

He responded with an emoji that had hearts for eyes.

Bailey started to type something else out but stopped herself. It was barely eight on a Saturday morning. She'd probably awakened him with her text in the first place. She cringed and hastily typed out,

"I'm sorry if I texted too early. Didn't even think to look at the clock."

She followed it with an embarrassed emoji.

"You're good. Minnie and I have already been on a walk. Text anytime. I'm always happy to hear from you."

The written words made her pulse jump, and that

brought a frown to her face. She sent a thumbs up and jammed the phone into her back pocket.

"Come on, guys. We need to go check on the ducks."

◦

"I hate to say it, but you may need to hire another person or two this season." Rachel tilted her head and fanned her face.

Even with the air conditioning going and several fans situated throughout the store, it still got warm when the space was filled with customers.

"I was thinking the same thing." If the rest of the fall season was this busy, Bailey didn't think she'd have much choice. "I'll go over the budget this week."

She'd add it to the list of things she needed to decide on when it came to the farm. With the kind of interest the place had gotten this year, expanding would be the smart move. It all felt so overwhelming, though. She and Joe had so many plans. Now, simply narrowing it all down to what exactly she should build on seemed like too much.

What Bailey needed to do was sit down and get specific with time, money, and options. Put together a pros and cons list. Maybe then the answer would be more obvious.

"Excuse me."

A woman's voice pulled Bailey out of her own head. An older lady held out her hand. "My grandson found this near the sunflower field. I wanted to make sure and turn it in. I figured someone might be looking for it."

She dropped a watch into Bailey's hand.

"I appreciate that. Thank you."

The customer smiled warmly and headed back outside.

Seth ran up. "Whoa. It's like a treasure. I wish I'd found

it." He rubbed a finger across the metal band. "Sure is dirty."

"I'm betting it's been out there for a while." Bailey ran a thumb over the watch face to dislodge the dried dirt. "The battery probably died some time ago." It wasn't an overly fancy watch, but it wasn't cheap, either. Based on the petite size, she guessed it'd been made for a woman's wrist.

"Are we going to find out who dropped it?"

"We're sure going to try."

A grin lit up Seth's face. "Just like detectives! Can I have it for a few minutes? I'll draw a picture of it and write down any clues I see."

"That would be great, sweetie. Thank you." She'd be taking photos of it, too, but she hated to deny her son the chance to indulge his creativity.

He beamed at her and carefully took the watch before going to the table where Jordan was playing.

"Isn't that something?" Rachel shook her head. "It had to have been dropped recently, or surely someone would've spotted it before now."

"One would think. I'll put a sign up on the bulletin board next weekend. Make sure someone identifies it if they claim they've lost a watch. Hopefully, we'll find the owner."

"I could take it to town for you this evening. Maybe run it down to the police station." Rachel motioned to the boys, who were both bent over the watch. "At least it would take one thing off your plate."

"I appreciate that, but I'll keep it here in case someone asks about it. I may even put up a couple of posts on Facebook and Instagram to see if someone speaks up about having lost it."

"Sounds like a good plan." Rachel gave her an encouraging smile. "I hope someone comes forward to claim it."

Bailey hoped so, too. They had a lost and found box, but she didn't want to put the watch in there. Someone might see it and just take it whether it belonged to them or not. If no one stepped forward, she would consider taking it to a jewelry store to see if it was worth anything. She knew next to nothing about watches or the different brands, but by the size of it, it clearly belonged to a woman.

The watch kept the boys entertained for a good half hour. When Seth brought it back to Bailey, she slipped it into a drawer in the small office area.

By the time the store closed to the public, she was exhausted and more than ready to go home. She said goodbye to Rachel and wished her a good week, then made sure everything was clean and put away. Finally, she got the watch out of the drawer, put it in her bag, and loaded the kids into the truck.

The boys were quarreling as Bailey drove them to the front gate. She retrieved the mail from the small box out front and tossed it into the passenger seat. Before going back through the gate, she activated the lock and waited for it to close again behind them.

"Mom! Jordan won't stop throwing his Batman." Seth was clearly done dealing with his little brother. No doubt he was stretching down to retrieve the action figure every time.

"Stop giving it back to him, and he'll figure it out."

They were halfway back to the house when Jordan started to cry.

Bailey swallowed a sigh. She enjoyed her sons so much, but she couldn't wait for bedtime tonight. There was a lot on her mind, and the chaos of the day was making it impossible to sort through any of it.

They finally stopped arguing when she set dinner on

the table. Once they had finished eating, they were back to being best friends. The sounds of their Hot Wheels track floated down the hall.

Thankful for the small break, she dove into the stack of mail. Most of it was trash. There were two bills, but it was the plain, white envelope with her name typed on it and no return address that caught her attention.

Bailey flattened the trifold piece of paper and began to read the typed note.

"Accept the next offer to buy your property. You will regret it if you don't."

The content was typed, and as she re-read the message, the air around her grew hot. She backed against a kitchen chair and sat down hard.

Chapter Seven

Nate ran a hand through his hair and watched with satisfaction as Corporal Conway walked to his car. Natty, a sweet German shepherd mix, trotted alongside him. If the way she kept looking at him were any indication, it would be the start of a beautiful friendship.

This was why he worked for Paws for a Cause. He was one of only three paid employees heading the non-profit organization that relied heavily on donations and volunteers. They all worked hard to train dogs who needed a second chance at a good home and match them with someone like a veteran or police officer who would benefit from the kind of therapy that only a furry companion could give.

When Corporal Conway first came in, he was hesitant and doubted that having a dog would help with anything at all. He'd only agreed to check it out at the insistence of his father.

But after three meetings where he and Natty were given time to interact, it was clear they were the perfect match. Corporal Conway said he was happy to be proven wrong.

Nate prayed that they'd be able to help each other heal from the wounds of their pasts.

He'd originally met Minnie through the program. The dog had brought him a great deal of joy, and not being home alone gave him the distraction he often needed to keep him from focusing on his last case before he left the police department.

Now, he enjoyed helping others find that same satisfaction and freedom.

Not for the first time, he thought about Bailey and how she would benefit from having a dog herself. It'd be good for the boys, too. Plus, it would provide an extra level of protection for all of them. Maybe one of these days, he'd be able to convince her to adopt one.

He headed home for the day. The moment he stepped through the front door, Minnie was there to greet him. Her docked tail wagged back and forth at top speed.

"Hey, girl. I missed you, too." He set his things down and joined her on the floor. "What do you think? Should we go for a walk? Or maybe play ball in the backyard?"

At the mention of ball, Minnie tilted her head to one side.

"Ball it is." He snatched a tennis ball from her box of toys and led the way outside. He'd only thrown it for her twice when his phone pinged with an incoming text.

Nate threw the ball across the yard and pulled his phone out. It was a group text that included him, Jenny, and Bailey.

"I got this in the mail today."

The message was from Bailey. A moment later, another text came through with a photo of a type-written letter. Nate clicked the image and increased the magnification so he could read the words.

If Nate were to actually hold the paper in his hand, he'd have a difficult time not crumpling it up and tossing it to the ground. That realtors were asking Bailey to sell her place was bad enough, but how dare someone have the audacity to send her a letter like this?

Combine the letter with the vandalism, and he didn't feel at all comfortable about the situation. Besides, he'd spent some time looking into her property and the realtor who had bothered her at work.

He texted her back.

> "I'll be right over."

His message barely went through when his phone pinged again with a response from Jenny.

> "Don't handle it any more than necessary. I'll come get it and take it back to the station."

Bailey's only response was,

> "Okay."

Minnie whined, her ball in her mouth and her eyes on Nate.

"Sorry, girl. I got distracted. How would you like to go play with Seth and Jordan? Where's your leash?"

The ball fell to the floor, completely forgotten, as she raced for the back door.

Nearly half an hour later, he put in the code to drive onto Thompson Family Farm. The sun was already beginning to set. Nate liked the cooling temperatures, but he didn't care for the shorter days that came with them.

He pulled into the driveway in front of Bailey's home to find that Jenny's patrol car was already there.

After getting out of his truck, he snapped a leash on Minnie and led her to the front door. It swung open before they'd reached it, and Bailey ushered them in.

Minnie's nub wagged double time as she greeted everyone. Seth and Jordan fawned all over her, and it wasn't clear whether they or the dog enjoyed it more. He took her leash off and kept an eye on her as the boys lavished her with pats and praise.

Jenny greeted Nate with a tight smile. "Hey, not that it isn't nice to see you more often, but we've got to stop meeting like this."

"Seriously." He looked to Bailey and offered her an encouraging smile.

Her brows were drawn, and the lines at the corners of her mouth deepened with the frown that quickly replaced the small smile she'd given him in return.

Jenny lifted a piece of paper that she'd slipped into a clear evidence bag. "I'll take it back and have the team check it for prints. Same with the envelope, especially the inside. Maybe they'll come up with something."

Bailey nodded, but she didn't look convinced. "I appreciate that." She glanced at her sons and lowered her voice. "I realize the letter is likely referencing the fact that if I don't accept the next offer, realtors won't stop bothering me, but it feels more sinister. As if I need to watch our backs."

Nate didn't care whether the threat was an empty one or not. It was messed up to send a letter like that to anyone.

Especially considering that Bailey was a widow trying to raise two little boys on her own.

He'd love to get this person alone in a room and teach him or her some proper manners.

Jenny turned to Nate. "I already told Bailey that I need to run. I'm having dinner with my parents in about forty-five minutes." She made a face.

"Uh oh. I take it that's not a good thing?"

"It entirely depends on whether it's a nice, relaxing family meal or if my mom has taken it upon herself to find the love of my life and present him as a blind date."

Bailey put an arm around her friend's shoulder. "I'll be praying for you. Call if you need to talk about it. Or text if you need an escape."

Jenny chuckled. "Will do, and I just might take you up on that last one." She sobered. "I'll run this letter by the station first. Seriously, Bailey. Just be extra careful, and call if you're worried about anything. Okay?"

"I will. Thanks again for coming out here."

Jenny waved goodbye and left, closing the door behind her.

Bailey walked over and turned the deadbolt in place. She leaned against the door and closed her eyes. When she opened them again, they were filled with a combination of exhaustion and worry.

"I wish I knew why someone was doing this. And why now? It doesn't make any sense."

Nate wished he had the perfect thing to say to make her feel more at ease. "I dug into the realtor who came to the store yesterday. He's sold property for many people, but he tends to specialize in large pieces of real estate, and he's been known to locate property and sell it to the town of Destiny."

Her brows rose as she pushed away from the door and motioned for him to follow her into the dining room. "Can I get you a Coke or Sprite?"

"I'll take a Sprite. Thank you." He waited until she'd handed a can to him and got one for herself. They sat down at the table where he could keep an eye on Minnie and make sure she wasn't getting too rowdy with the boys—or vice versa.

Nate took a sip of his soda. "Destiny has been growing a lot, and the city limits have been expanding steadily for a while. This area out here is probably the next to be transformed into residential property, and a place like yours could bring in a lot of money if it were sectioned off and sold as plots for developers. It could be that someone is trying to capitalize on that. Buy from you now when it would be cheaper and then sell when the land is in high demand in a few more years. Maybe even less."

It wasn't a bad business plan and one that he could respect if it were all done on the up-and-up. But sending a threatening letter to the owner in hopes of scaring her into selling was inexcusable. Of course, there was no proof that Mr. Driver had anything to do with the letter at all.

Bailey looked thoughtful, but she didn't say anything.

He picked up his can of soda. "If you remember the names of any of the realtors who've contacted you, please let me know. I'd like to check on their companies, too. It's also possible that there may be some mineral rights interests. If someone thinks there may be a good source of oil or something similar, they may be hoping to purchase the land specifically to sell the mineral rights to another company."

"How do we find out about that?"

"I'll do more digging."

"I appreciate it." Bailey took a long drink of her Sprite.

Minnie ran into the dining room and dove beneath the table, shaking his soda can along with the salt and pepper shakers.

Jordan squealed and started to duck under the table when Bailey reached out and snagged him by the arm. "I don't think so, mister. You're going to knock this table over and make a mess."

Nate snapped his fingers to get Minnie's attention. She crawled out again, a guilty look on her face, and came to sit by his chair. He might have laughed at the penitent look on her face if it wouldn't have taken away from Bailey's discussion with Jordan.

Seth stood nearby and watched the exchange while the younger boy's chin dropped.

"Sorry, Mama."

"I'm not angry. I just need you to be more careful." Bailey reached for her youngest son and gave him a reassuring hug.

"I will." He wiggled out of the hug and turned to look at Nate. "Can I still play with Minnie if we don't run?"

Nate glanced at Bailey, whose expression was open even though she looked exhausted.

"If it's okay with your mom, why don't you and Seth go watch some cartoons. If you sit on the floor by the couch, Minnie will come and sit with you. Then you can spend time together without getting too riled up. How does that sound?"

Jordan's eyes brightened. "Can we, Mama?"

Seth didn't say anything, but he looked hopeful.

"I think that's a great idea." Bailey held up her first and second fingers. "Two episodes. And then you need to start getting ready for your baths and bed."

"Yes, ma'am." The words barely left Seth's lips before

he'd turned and walked as quickly as possible back into the living room. Jordan followed, and Minnie trotted after them.

Nate chuckled. "They could use a dog of their own. It'd be good for them."

When he looked over to see what she thought of the idea, he found her massaging her temples, her elbows resting on the table.

"Hey." Nate reached across the table and lightly touched her arm. "We're going to figure this out."

"There's just a lot. Trying to keep the store running while keeping track of the boys. Then there's wondering whether I should leave the farm as is, expand, or sell." When she raised her head and opened her eyes, there was no missing the guilt there. "I don't need someone threatening my family on top of it."

Her chin quivered slightly as tears filled her eyes. She blinked them back as though her very survival depended on not allowing a single one to fall.

Chapter Eight

Bailey refused to cry in front of Nate. Not to mention, the boys could run back in any minute and see her upset. Sometimes, it felt like everything since Joe died had been hard. Everything. She'd made a promise to herself that she'd take care of the boys and do her best, and that's exactly what she'd done. She'd push through this just like she'd made it through everything else the last two years.

She had to.

Nate's voice dragged her gaze to his face.

"Talk to me, Bailey. Let me be your sounding board. Maybe it'll help you at least prioritize what you need to do. Sometimes, having a set list of priorities makes all the difference."

She glanced down to where his hand was still resting on her arm, his fingers warm against her skin. His thumb lightly brushed her arm twice before he moved his hand. Bailey tried to ignore how she instantly missed the touch.

He was right, though. She needed to get this straightened out in her mind. As it was, every evening, she was so mentally exhausted that she'd put it off until the next day. Her mom used to call it mental paralysis when you were so overwhelmed that your brain just called it quits and wouldn't allow you to focus on anything.

That's where Bailey was right now. Maybe having Nate here and being forced to list and go through the options was exactly what she needed.

"Yeah. Okay. Let me go grab my notebook." She'd left it on the side table in the living room where she was going to go through things last night.

As she rounded the couch, the image of the boys sitting on the floor, Minnie curled up between them, had her snapping a picture of them with her phone.

Nate was right. A dog would be good for them, but the thought of taking on another living creature that depended on her to stay alive sounded like too much right now.

She returned to the kitchen table and showed Nate the picture before sitting back down across from him. She took the pen off the notebook spiral and opened to the second section. The page was covered with questions.

Nate gave her his full attention and waited for her to start.

Bailey took a deep breath and intentionally looked away from the wall of handwriting. "We're getting busy enough this fall that I'm going to have to hire at least one more person to help Rachel and me. Maybe two. As it is now, it's nearly impossible to manage things and keep an eye on the boys." She lowered her voice. "You know how Jordan is. I turn my back for a second, and he disappears. I don't even want to know what it'll be like next fall when Seth starts kindergarten and Jordan has no one to play with." Seth barely missed the cutoff to start going to school this year. Realistically, Jordan would be a year older and maybe a bit more mature then, but she couldn't rely on that. He'd been one to run off ever since he was old enough to be on his feet.

"Hiring another person or two makes sense. It would help Rachel out and make it easier for you to be more flexible. You could hang out with the boys or wander around the farm more to interact with your guests." He leaned his chair back. "Do you have enough money coming in to hire two more people without putting stress on the finances?"

She nodded. "We'd be fine, at least for a while. That leads to my next set of questions, which are much harder to answer." With one finger, she traced the border of the page in front of her. "Joe and I had talked about expanding the area of the farm that's open to the public. Turn this place into a big attraction in the fall with a corn maze, hay rides, a playground, and a large pumpkin patch."

Nate looked interested, and he leaned forward again, the chair righting itself. "Wow, that would be amazing. What would it take to get to that point?"

"There's the old barn a couple of acres to the north through the trees. It's an eyesore, and honestly, we were both worried about it being a safety hazard. Now that the boys are getting bigger, it feels like a matter of time before they try to explore and wind up getting hurt. Especially Seth. He's obsessed with it." Her hair, which she'd put into a messy bun that morning, was coming loose on one side. Several strands of hair hung by her ear, and she twirled them around one finger. "I'm thinking of having the whole thing torn down and hauled off. Then we could section that area off for a corn maze."

She could picture it in her mind and see her boys running hand in hand as they tried to find the exit. If much of the area was already cleared, it would make that part easier. She'd just have to research drainage and what it would take to grow that amount of corn. More items for her to-do list, but she'd get to that once a decision was made.

Bailey shrugged. "It's going to take all winter and spring to do everything necessary, and it may even take most of next fall to get the corn and another pumpkin patch established. We might be looking at two years from now before we open that area to the public. So, you see why I need to make a decision and start moving forward. Talking about it is just the beginning."

Nate nodded. "You'll need to put costs together. See how long it might take to cover that investment and eventually turn a profit."

"Exactly. Right now, we pretty much rely on purchases. But once everything is in place, if there are enough activities, I'm hoping we can have a flat charge for admission. That, in combination with purchases, will hopefully bring in a lot more."

"It's a solid plan. Why are you hesitating?" Nate folded his hands and laid them on the table, his expression open.

For the second time that evening, tears flooded her eyes, no matter how hard she tried to will them away.

"Because Joe and I were supposed to do it together." The words came out as more of a whisper. She gave a shrug and swiped at a lone tear that escaped. "This was his dream, you know. He wanted this for our family. He hoped to retire early, and then we could run the farm with the boys. Joe had all these plans..."

She didn't dare look at Nate. She didn't want him to feel sorry for her. It'd been over two years, yet Joe's death left a hole in her heart that would never close completely. She had to figure out how *she* was going to manage things going forward.

"There are no words adequate to tell you how I wish

things had been different for you two." Nate's voice was gruff. "You mentioned selling the place earlier. Is that something you're seriously considering?"

She wished she hadn't said that at all. She'd been upset, and it'd slipped out. "Sometimes, when it feels overwhelming, I think about the possibility. But it's just when I'm at the end of the day and exhausted. You know?"

"Bailey."

Silence. When she finally lifted her chin, Nate wasn't looking at her with pity—only understanding and determination crossed his face. "It doesn't make you a bad person."

She shook her head. Her chest tightened, and she wanted to object but said nothing.

"Guilt can wreck your life." He cleared his throat. "Trust me, I know."

Chapter Nine

Nate could see the guilt in Bailey's eyes. It was an emotion he knew well, just like he knew how paralyzing and devastating it could be. He still fought at times to keep it from taking control of his life.

His feelings toward Bailey alone ate him up with guilt on a regular basis. It was an old case he'd worked on, though, that had led him to seek out grief counseling after it ended in the worst way possible. Therapy had helped, but sometimes, that guilt reared up when he least expected it. He suspected it always would.

The cause of his guilt was very different from what Bailey was experiencing, but the result was the same.

Another tear slid from the corner of her eye and started to roll down her cheek. It took everything in him not to reach out and wipe it away for her. He said a silent prayer, asking that God would give him the words to say. Words that might help her but wouldn't reveal how he felt or make anything harder for her.

She glanced toward the living room as though she were

afraid the boys might see her cry. When she looked back at Nate, he plunged ahead.

"I want to tell you something, and I need you to hear me out."

Her eyes narrowed with doubt and a hint of apprehension.

"Joe loved you and the boys fiercely. He would want nothing more than for you to be happy. That would be true whether you transform this place into something people come from miles around to see or if you sell it all and decide to live in an apartment." He paused for a moment to let that sink in. "There's no doubt in my mind that Joe would be proud of you and of the way you're raising Seth and Jordan."

He meant every word, too. *He* was proud of her. She'd been through so much in the last two years, and she'd faced it all with grace and courage. Nate doubted he could've handled it as well.

He wasn't sure what kind of reaction he expected from her. She hastily stood from the table and went to the sink to look out the window, and he couldn't tell if she was upset or not. He contemplated waiting for her to return, but when her chin dropped, and she leaned into the counter, he strode across the room to stand behind her.

Every instinct told him to put an arm around her—to offer her some kind of comfort. Instead, his feet stayed rooted in place, his arms pressed against his sides.

"I should have kept my mouth shut. I'm sorry if I upset you." It was the last thing he'd wanted to do. "Bailey..." He finally reached out and gently cupped her elbow.

She turned around, met his eyes just long enough for him to register the tears that had finally pushed past their barriers, and stepped into his arms. It wasn't until her arms went around his waist and clasped behind his back that his shock wore off enough to react.

Nate held her gently, his right hand rubbing small circles on her back that he hoped were calming. Comforting. The scent of her shampoo—something soft and floral—filled his senses. He registered the way she so perfectly fit against his chest, her head at the right height to press a kiss to.

If she'd been his to kiss.

Instead, he rested his cheek against her soft hair and let her cry. Her sobs were silent, and if he hadn't been able to feel the ragged breaths that came with her emotion, he wouldn't have known. Certainly, the boys had no idea that their mother was struggling.

He reached for a paper towel on the counter nearby and handed it to her. She gave him a slight nod in response and dabbed at her face.

Finally, she rested her forehead against his chest. "I'm sorry. I don't usually fall apart like that..." she ended the words with a frustrated sigh.

Nate cupped her face with one hand and gently lifted her chin until she was looking up at him. "Are you kidding? You're the strongest, bravest person I've ever known. This doesn't change a thing."

When another tear left the corner of her eye, he didn't hesitate to swipe it away this time. Even with puffy eyes and a red nose from crying, she was the most beautiful woman he'd ever seen. His heart tumbled painfully in his chest.

She stilled as she studied his face. The trust in her eyes nearly did him in.

Seth's voice floated in from the living room. "Mom? I'm hungry!"

The words acted like a jolt of electricity, and Nate

immediately dropped his hand. Bailey blinked and took a step back.

There was that familiar guilt again. He'd nearly allowed himself to slip up and give her an idea of how he felt about her. Something he'd promised himself he would never do.

He forced a chuckle. "I remember thinking I was starving to death nearly my whole childhood. I'm convinced boys are born with an extra stomach." Nate prayed he sounded normal.

"I have no doubt that's true." Bailey rubbed the palms of her hands on her pants and turned toward the living room. "I'll make you a snack in a few minutes."

"Okay!" The single word was followed by silence as Seth probably focused on the cartoon again.

Bailey walked back to the table and took a seat. She reached for her pencil and let the eraser bounce off the notebook several times.

He rejoined her and thought through everything they'd spoken about before. "It sounds like, no matter what you decide to do, the old barn is a concern. So start there. Have it torn down and the area leveled. At least then you won't be worried about the boys getting hurt or someone else messing with the building."

She nodded slowly. "That's a good idea. Even if I sold the place, that would only increase the value. No one wants to mess with a derelict building that could potentially be a hazard." She made some notes at the bottom of the page. "I'll call around tomorrow and see who might do that kind of thing. Get some quotes."

"At least it'll be a start. Then you can decide what to do afterward. In the end, whatever you think is the best thing for you and the boys is the right decision. Don't let anyone else tell you otherwise."

That included her own conscience, although he kept that to himself.

"I appreciate that." When she looked over at him, her cheeks had turned a light shade of pink, and there was a hint of embarrassment in her eyes. "Now, if things would calm down a little around here, that would be great. We've had enough excitement for a while."

The kids' show must have ended because they, along with Minnie, wandered into the kitchen.

"What are we having for snack?" Seth held a hand over his stomach for emphasis.

Jordan looped an arm around Minnie's neck and gave her a hug. "We're hungry, too."

Minnie panted while she watched the adults with interest, almost as though she, too, were asking for food.

Nate chuckled. "We'll get out of your hair and let you guys get to your evening routine." He snapped his fingers, and Minnie moved to stand beside him. Both boys ran over to give Nate a hug goodbye. "You two, be sure to help your mom out, okay?"

Jordan looked up at Nate. "Can you bring Minnie back next time you come over?"

"We'll see." Nate ruffled the boy's hair.

Bailey followed him to the front door, where he turned and lowered his voice. "Be careful. Don't forget to call me if you need anything."

"I will." The corners of her mouth tugged upward as a little sparkle returned to her eyes. "Thanks again."

There was nothing else to do but give her and the boys a wave and lead Minnie out to his truck. He said a prayer over them as her place faded in the rearview mirror. And then, as he had many times before, he asked God to help his feelings for Bailey to fade away.

Chapter Ten

Bailey was thankful that the worship service at church was filled with lively music this Sunday. It'd taken a while to fall asleep last night, and then several dreams had awakened her up with a start. Each time, it took over a half hour to go back to sleep again.

By the time her alarm went off this morning, she was starting to wonder if she'd have been better off pulling an all-nighter. Then, at least the lack of sleep would've been on her terms.

Jordan leaned against her leg. She reached down and lifted him into her arms, where he laid his head on her shoulder. It wouldn't be long before he'd be too big to hold like this, and church was about the only place where he was calm enough to give her the opportunity.

When worship ended, she watched to make sure her boys connected with their Sunday school teachers and then took a seat, suddenly feeling very alone. Funny how even the air around her felt colder than it had before.

She noted how the couple in the row ahead of her were sitting close together, his arm across the back of her chair. A pang of longing hit her hard. The last thing she needed was to cry at church.

Bailey grabbed the bulletin and looked it over, the words blurring in front of her. Crying in front of Nate last night was bad enough, but then she had to go and lose her cool while in his arms. What on Earth? The memory made her face warm.

She wasn't sure what had come over her, only that she had the sudden need to be held and comforted.

And Nate? He'd been amazing—with the right combination of patience, encouragement, and candor that she needed.

She'd always considered Nate a friend, but since Joe's death, he'd really stepped up to help her and the boys. For a moment last night, there'd been something in his eyes that made her pulse speed up. Something that made her question everything about their friendship, and then it was gone as quickly as it'd appeared.

Now, she was almost sure she'd been imagining things. Which was far more dangerous because when she realized she'd misunderstood him last night, there was a twinge of disappointment.

Nate was right. Joe would want her to be happy. To move forward and live her life. That probably included sharing her life with another man at some point, but that wasn't something she was ready to think about yet. Certainly not with Joe's best friend.

Not that he was interested in her like that.

She forced her thoughts and attention back on the message and made notes to keep herself on track. When the sermon was over, Bailey looked up to see Gabe and Paige Harrison at the end of the aisle. Paige caught her eye and smiled.

Bailey gathered her things and welcomed a hug from Paige. She and Gabe, another police officer with the Destiny PD, were married a few months ago in a beautiful ceremony that even included his canine partner, Loki.

"It's good to see you both. How's married life treating you?"

Paige looked up at her husband with a smile on her face and a slight blush on her cheeks. "It's been good." The sweet look was replaced with one of concern when she turned back to Bailey. "How have *you* been? We've been keeping you and the boys in our prayers."

Gabe nodded. "I'm sorry for the trouble at your place this last week. I'm glad to hear you've been in touch with Jenny and Nate. If there's anything any of us at the station can do for you, please don't hesitate to ask."

That was one thing Bailey had discovered when she'd married Joe: The officers at the PD were like a family of their own. They looked out for one another, and she was thankful for that.

Joe's parents lived on the East Coast. Even before he'd died, they saw them once a year at Christmas, and that had continued to be the case. Her own parents had passed away years ago; they'd never been close, and she had no siblings.

If it weren't for the Destiny PD family, she didn't know what she would've done. It was probably three months after the funeral before she had to go grocery shopping or start cooking her own meals again.

"I appreciate that. Thank you."

She said goodbye to the couple, made small talk with several other people on her way to the classrooms, and then picked up the boys.

As she often did on Sundays, she went through a drive-through on the way home to get a couple of kids' meals and a chicken sandwich before heading home. The scents filled the truck and made Bailey's mouth water. She hadn't eaten breakfast and regretted that decision partway through worship.

They were singing along with a soundtrack from one of the boys' favorite Disney movies when they approached the front gate to the farm. Bailey's foot nearly slipped off the brake when she noticed the large, red FOR SALE sign that had been nailed onto the post out front. Instead of a phone number below, it said, "See owner for details."

Anger filled her as she rolled the window down to punch in the passcode. What she wanted to do was get out of the truck and rip the sign right off the post, but she'd watched enough police procedural shows to wonder if there might be fingerprints left behind. She snapped a photo with her phone and did her best to rejoin the boys in song as she drove through the gates.

She didn't want to interrupt Nate or Jenny on a Sunday if they had the day off. She'd call the police station and report the for sale sign to whoever was on duty.

The road led past the sizable parking area and around to the country store.

Bailey was about to continue around the bend when something about the store snagged her attention. The two large flowerpots on either side of the front door had been knocked over.

Her stomach knotted, and the pangs of hunger were replaced with churning dread.

"Boys, I need to check on something really quick before we head home."

"But I'm hungry!"

"Can't we eat first?"

"That's enough." Her firm voice, a tone reserved for

serious situations, silenced the objections. She pulled to a stop in front of the shop. "I'll be right back. Stay in the truck."

As much as she wanted to hope that something natural had knocked the pots over, she knew that wasn't the case. Even when they had a terrible thunderstorm roll through a year ago with record-breaking winds, the heavy planters stood strong.

Bailey placed a hand on the gun tucked into a holster at her waist. Once they purchased the farm, she'd gotten to where she didn't go anywhere without it.

She ascended the four steps onto the deck and cautiously approached the front door.

The pots hadn't just been knocked over. They'd been smashed to pieces. Now that she was closer, every single window had been shattered as well.

The door itself wasn't closed completely, but she didn't pull it open. Instead, she cupped her hand against the window and peered inside.

Everything she could see was in disarray from a display shelf across the way to the checkout counter.

Tears of anger burned her eyes, and fear coursed through her. She clenched a fist as she jogged back to the truck. With a deep breath, she turned to look at her sons.

"Boys, someone broke into the shop and made a real mess of everything. We're going to need to call the police and stay here until they arrive." Before Seth got too worried or they started to complain about being hungry, she raised a hand to stop them. "You can eat your lunch here in the truck while we wait."

Eating in vehicles was something she'd forbidden since Seth was little because it always ended up in a colossal mess. Both boys' eyes widened in disbelief.

"Really?" Seth looked at his little brother. "Can we still have ketchup for our fries?"

Even if the boys did their worst on purpose, the mess in the truck couldn't even begin to compare to what she was going to have to deal with inside the store.

"Yes, you can still have ketchup for your fries."

"Yay!" Jordan's excitement was impossible to miss. Seth seemed happy with the idea, but there was a shadow of worry on his face, too.

"Everything's going to be fine. I'm going to call the police so they can take pictures, and we'll just eat our lunch while we wait." She gave her oldest a smile to reassure him. As quickly as she could, she got their meals set up and carefully handed the food to them. "I'm going to step right outside to make that call. You two be careful not to make a mess."

The boys only nodded as they began to devour their food.

She left the truck's engine running so the boys would stay cool. With one eye on the door to the store, she dialed the Destiny Police Department.

Chapter Eleven

By the time Nate arrived at Thompson Family Farm, Destiny PD had cleared the store, and Bailey had started to walk through the building to see if anything had been stolen. From what little he'd seen of the interior, it might be difficult to determine if anything had been taken. Displays had been knocked over, drawers dumped onto the floor, and even the pictures on the wall had been ripped off and smashed. Combine that with the FOR SALE sign on the front gate, and it was clear someone was getting bolder. Not a good thing.

He was grateful he had Seth and Jordan and their game of cornhole to keep him distracted because he was *angry*. Mostly, he was upset that someone had once again targeted Bailey and her family, but he was also frustrated with her. He had to find out about the vandalism from a friend of a friend. After yesterday, he couldn't understand why she hadn't called him.

When he arrived, two police cars were already at the store. Bailey spotted him and gave him a look that ping-ponged between relief and guilt. He'd volunteered to keep the boys occupied and hadn't had the chance to talk to her yet.

Seth retrieved the bean bags and handed the blue ones to Jordan. "Let's play again." He motioned toward the corn-hole board. "You go first, Jordan. You can stand closer if you want to."

Jordan dropped the four blue bean bags on the ground at his feet, then reached down to grasp one with his chubby little hand. With his tongue peeking out in concentration, the first one he threw didn't come near the hole. The brothers took turns tossing their bean bags until they were out.

"You two are getting good at this." Nate walked over and counted the bags that had gone in the hole as well as those that had landed on the board. "Seth won by two, but you're getting better every time, Jordan. Do you guys want to play again?"

"Nah." Seth wrinkled his nose and flopped onto a wooden picnic table bench. Several of them were arranged in the area outside the store. He looked at the door and frowned. "How much longer do you think it'll be?"

"I wish I knew, buddy. They're going as fast as they can in there."

Another car pulled into the parking lot. Nate waved as Jenny got out and walked over. She put a hand on Jordan's head. "Hey, guys. You staying busy?"

"We're trying." Nate raised an eyebrow.

Jordan set his bean bags on the picnic table. "I wanna go home."

"I bet you do." She nodded toward the store. "I've got these guys. Why don't you go see how it's going?"

"You sure?" Nate really didn't mind sitting with the

boys, but he would like to find out where they were in the investigation and make sure Bailey was okay.

"Absolutely. We're good."

"Thanks, Jenny." He slapped the top of the picnic table with one hand and turned to go inside. There were two different officers taking photographs of the damage.

Detective John Paris was talking to Bailey in the back of the store. Nate picked his way through the mess on the floor until he reached them.

"Walker." Detective Paris gave Nate a nod. "Good to see you."

"You, too." Nate looked from him to Bailey. "I'm so sorry this happened to you. Have you guys made any headway on finding out who's responsible?"

"Not yet, unfortunately." Paris frowned. "It looks like they came in through the front door. Most likely using a crowbar. Officers have dusted for prints, but given the number of people who come in and out, it's going to be hard to know which prints to focus on."

"I knew I should've installed cameras. They just seemed so unnecessary at the time." Regret tinged Bailey's voice as she crossed her arms in front of her. "It's going to take forever to get this cleaned up. I'll be lucky if I'm able to re-open the store before the end of the season." She leaned against a nearby display and picked at her bottom lip.

Nate wanted to encourage her, but there was no denying how much of a mess the place was. "Can you tell if anything is missing?"

"If they took something, it's not obvious. I don't leave money here overnight, and I make sure to take home anything personal. This feels...vindictive." Her chin rose. "Did you see the for sale sign that someone put out front?"

"Yep. I have a hard time believing that two separate

individuals decided to mess with your place on the same day. They must be connected."

Paris nodded. "I agree." He motioned to the chaos around them. "Between the damage to your goat pen and now this... They're clearly trying to send you a message."

"I don't like being pushed around. This is extreme and a big jump from destroying a fence." The muscles in Bailey's jaw flexed.

Nate wondered the same thing. This was escalating fast, and he worried about Bailey and the boys.

Paris looked over his notes. "They might have trashed the place so that it's harder to see what was stolen. Or maybe it's a disgruntled customer? Even if it's directly related to someone wanting to buy your place, this kind of damage would suggest it's not to purchase the business itself."

That made sense. Most people wouldn't damage what they were trying to obtain. If Bailey wasn't able to get all of this cleaned up in time to open on Friday, then she'd have to let customers know. It could potentially harm the business longterm, which would be counterproductive if that's why someone wanted the place.

Man, he wished she didn't live out here alone like this.

The detective must have been thinking along the same lines as he spoke to Bailey. "I'll have patrols drive by regularly for the next few days. That said, your property is large. It would be a good idea to install cameras around your home and the store if you can. Anything to deter someone from coming on your land. Sometimes even putting up warning signs about home security will help because it's just enough to make a would-be thief second guess breaking into your home."

Nate noticed the way Bailey shivered and wrapped her arms around herself.

She gave a barely perceptible nod. "Thanks. I'm going to check on the boys. Then I guess I'd better start going through everything so I have some numbers for the insurance company tomorrow." With that, she moved toward the door.

Nate waited until she was outside before speaking with Paris again. "I'm worried about them. Whoever's behind this is getting bold. Dangerous."

"I tend to agree with you. This is officially my case now, and I intend to do everything I can to figure out who's behind this. In the meantime, you might encourage Bailey to take the boys and stay with family or friends. Just until things quiet down a little."

"I'll do what I can, but she's not the type to back down." It was a personality trait of hers that he normally admired greatly.

"I get it. Trust me. Eve's like that. Won't back down until she's solved the problem. Then again, she says the same about me." He chuckled. "At least we can't hold it against each other."

"Very true." Nate laughed.

Detective Paris and the county's medical examiner, Eve Marks, started dating back in April, though they'd been friends for some time before that. It wasn't until they worked on a case that involved a serial killer who'd set his sights on Eve that they realized how they felt about each other. If Nate were a betting man, he'd wager that Paris would pop the question by the end of the year.

"We'll have officers finish cataloging photos of any evidence they find. Then I'll have a couple of them go around the perimeter of the farm. See if there's any obvious point where the trespasser is gaining access to the property. We'll check the for sale sign for fingerprints, too." He pocketed his notebook. "If Bailey isn't willing to leave her home, maybe a relative can come stay with her. I really don't like the idea of her being out here with the boys alone."

"Neither do I."

The problem was that she had no family in the area, and she wasn't overly close to the family she did have. There was no way Bailey would call them up and ask them to travel to Destiny.

He had an idea, but he wanted to talk to Jenny in case his first choice of options fell through. One way or another, he had to figure out a way to convince Bailey to let someone stay with her for a few days.

Chapter Twelve

The last of the police officers left with Detective Paris's promise that they'd do everything they could to figure out who was causing so much trouble. It made Bailey feel better that someone was actively investigating the case. Between all of the pictures and evidence the officers gathered, dusting the FOR SALE sign for prints, and checking the perimeter of the property, hopefully, they'd find some information that might help.

All in all, they'd spent several hours at the store. Now, it was well after four in the afternoon, and she needed to get the boys home. Hopefully, they'd go to bed easily tonight. She was exhausted and really needed them to. Desperately. Once they were asleep, she had every intention of digging into her candy stash. Something with peanut butter and chocolate was exactly what she needed after a day like today.

She looked at the notepad where she'd been making a list of things she needed to do. Like calling Rachel and letting her know the store might not be open to the public on Friday. Along with that, she planned to research companies who might be able to demolish the old barn, look into installing security cameras, and call her insurance company.

Not to mention the time it would take to get the shop itself cleaned up. That thought alone was overwhelming.

Maybe the company she hired to demolish the barn could do the same with the shop. Then, she could start over with a clean slate. Okay, not really, but the thought had crossed her mind in a flash of morbid humor.

While the police had been investigating, Nate and a couple of other guys she didn't know got a new door installed and boarded up the broken windows.

At least the store was secure again. Of course, she'd thought it was originally, too.

A touch to her arm made her jump. She slapped a hand against her chest and turned.

Jenny gave her an apologetic look. "I'm sorry. I was talking to you, and I didn't realize you hadn't heard me."

Bailey shook her head. "I guess I was lost in thought. What did you say?" She took a deep breath and sent up a silent prayer. *Lord, please give me the energy and focus to get through the rest of today.*

Nate stepped up beside Jenny, and the two of them exchanged looks.

Bailey's brows rose. "What's going on?"

Jenny cleared her throat. "We've been talking, and we're both worried about you and the boys being at the house alone tonight."

Bailey wasn't about to let someone run her out of her own home. That said, it was impossible to ignore the fact that if someone had gotten into the store easily, it wouldn't take much more to break into her house.

The thought made her stomach churn. She'd already decided to sleep in the living room so she could hear if anyone messed with the doors. The decision made her feel slightly better.

"We'll be okay," she told her friends, hoping she sounded more confident than she felt. "I appreciate it, though. I can't thank you both enough for everything you've done over the last few days."

Nate didn't look convinced. "Is there anyone you three could stay with for the next few days? I could run out here first thing to check on the animals for you."

"I'm not leaving my house." Bailey straightened her spine and crossed her arms. "It's the principle of the thing. I will not allow someone to run me off my own property." Surely they could understand that.

Judging by the look the two of them exchanged, they had not only expected her response but had a backup plan.

Bailey's eyes narrowed. "Why do I feel like you guys are conspiring behind my back?"

Jenny reached a comforting hand out and rested it on Bailey's arm. "Nate or I would like to stay with you for a few days. Another set of eyes can't hurt, and having another person present might be enough to deter someone from bothering you again. If you'd be more comfortable with me staying, I'm happy to do that." She motioned toward Nate. "But I'd prefer it if you let Nate be the one. He can bring Minnie with him, and she'll let you guys know if anyone is snooping around." She held up a hand to stop Bailey when she opened her mouth to object. "If they're keeping an eye on you, it'd be good for them to see a man around, not to mention a Rottweiler. There's no downside to this."

Bailey looked from one of her friends to the other. "You're serious." They'd clearly discussed this, and from the determined look on Nate's face, he agreed. She focused on him. "What about your job? You've got more important things to do than babysit us."

A muscle in his jaw flexed as he leveled her with an intense look. "First of all, there isn't much that's more important than making sure my friend and her boys are safe." He raised his eyebrows as though he dared her to contradict him. "Secondly, my boss has been on my case about taking some of my vacation time before I start losing it. I've got this entire week off."

"I can't let you spend your vacation here. There has got to be something else you'd rather be doing." She spoke the words, but her conviction was wavering. It was clear her friends had already put their plan into motion, and they weren't going to back down until she saw things their way.

Nate shrugged. "Not a thing. I intend to keep an eye on your place, Bailey. I can do that from inside your house, or I can camp out in the front yard."

"You can't be serious."

Jenny chuckled. "Oh, we're very serious. Except Nate and I would take turns watching your place out front. Tag team it, you know?"

Bailey rolled her eyes with a heavy sigh. She looked over at her boys, who were sitting at the picnic table. Jordan was driving a toy car around the top of the table, but Seth was clearly listening to the conversation.

"You two aren't going to let this go, are you?"

"Nope." Jenny perched her hands on her hips.

Nate gave her that smile that told her he knew he'd already won. "Not gonna happen."

"Fine." Bailey threw her hands in the air. "But I guarantee you, twenty-four hours in my house, and you'll be more than ready to go home again."

His lips lifted in an almost boyish grin—one that traveled all the way to his dark eyes. He motioned toward the parking lot. "In that case, I'm going to run home and pack a bag, get a few supplies, and Minnie and I will be back as soon as possible."

Jenny leaned against one of the poles that supported the awning overhead. "I'll stick around until you get back."

With that, Nate waved to the boys and jogged back to his truck.

Bailey pinned her friend with a stern look. "I can't believe the two of you conspired behind my back like that."

"We knew you wouldn't go along with it unless we had it all figured out first." She tossed some hair over her shoulder. "Tell me I'm wrong."

As much as Bailey wanted to, she couldn't. Because if their roles had been reversed, she wouldn't have hesitated to help either of them in a similar manner. "Thank you."

"You're welcome. It was Nate's idea. He didn't like the idea of the three of you being out here alone. I didn't either." She hesitated. "He really hoped you'd agree to let him stay."

"I hate that he feels obligated to keep checking on us."

At her words, Jenny's brows rose. "Obligated? You really have no idea, do you?"

"What do you mean?"

Jenny shook her head. "Come on. Let's get the boys back to your house. I'll help you get dinner ready for a seat at the table before I head back out."

Bailey laughed at that. "I'll take you up on that deal."

She finished closing the store, but Jenny's words kept going through her mind. What had she been talking about? Bailey had no idea about what?

It bothered her that Nate gave up his vacation to stay at

the house, but she couldn't deny that it'd be nice to have someone else around after everything that had happened. Vandalizing the goat pen was bad enough, but tearing the shop apart was on a whole different level. How far was someone willing to go to get her to sell her place?

Chapter Thirteen

When Nate got back to Bailey's house, she and Jenny had an early dinner ready. The chili dogs and chips tasted fantastic. It'd been a while since he'd last had a decent chili dog, and he'd had to stop himself from eating a fourth.

The five of them relaxed and talked about easy topics like Minecraft, catching bugs, and their favorite desserts.

After they were done eating, Jenny helped Bailey clean up the kitchen while Nate took the boys outside to throw the ball for Minnie. She liked it even better when Seth and Jordan ran after her, the joy evident on her face. She galloped across the yard just fast enough to stay out of arm's reach but slow enough to encourage Jordan to keep up the chase.

Bailey's laughter reached Nate's ears from the back porch where both women were now sitting. He wanted to join them but played with the boys and Minnie for a few more minutes until the Rottweiler collapsed on the grass, her tongue hanging.

Even Seth and Jordan looked tired. Hopefully, they'd

have no problem going to sleep tonight. Another glance at Bailey earned Nate a subtle nod of approval, which sent warmth through his chest.

It probably would've been smarter if he'd encouraged Jenny to stay with Bailey instead of taking on the job himself. But then, he would've been worried enough to camp out in front of her place anyway to keep an eye out for trespassers.

No, this was exactly where he needed to be. Spending extra time with Bailey, especially, wasn't exactly a bad thing, even if it made it harder to keep his feelings in check. He never would've doubted that until he'd nearly slipped up yesterday.

He was here to keep an eye on the place and make sure Bailey and the boys stayed safe until the police department could figure out who was trying to get her to sell and why.

Nate walked up the steps to the porch and leaned against the railing. "It's a good thing I didn't have to run. I ate way too many chili dogs." He patted his full stomach.

"Well, it looks like you got all three of them properly worn out." Jenny tilted her head toward the dog and the two boys who were sitting next to her on the grass. "That's seriously adorable."

"Yeah, it is." Bailey smiled again, the dimple in her right cheek winking. "Did I ever tell you guys that Seth once tried to bring Petunia into the house to stay in his room for the night? He insisted that she could be house-trained just like a dog." She laughed hard.

"That doesn't surprise me." Jenny shook her head. "That boy's going to grow up to be a lawyer or something the way he can argue his point."

They all laughed some more, but the mood quickly sobered.

"I wish we could've found Petunia." Bailey frowned. "I suppose we'll never know what happened to her, will we?"

That bothered Nate, too. Granted, the goats weren't house pets like Minnie was, but if Minnie had gone missing, it would bother Nate every day wondering where she was and whether she was being taken care of. "How's Poppy doing? Is her wound healing well?"

"No complications, and at least Pansy found her way back. That's something."

They sat in companionable silence for several minutes until Jenny moved to stand. "I should probably get out of your hair and get home. It's my sister's birthday today, so I need to call her tonight before it gets much later. If anything comes up and you need extra help, don't hesitate to call me. I'm serious."

Bailey stepped forward to give Jenny a hug. "I will. Thanks again for everything."

"Of course. Be careful, okay?"

Jenny flashed Nate a knowing look. "Keep me updated."

"Will do. Take care of yourself."

She nodded and then went to say goodbye to the boys before heading for her car and driving away.

It was starting to get dark, and Nate was about to suggest they go inside when Bailey addressed her sons.

"Come on, guys. It's bath time." She waved them inside, and Nate brought up the rear, closing and locking the door behind him.

Minnie trotted to the living room and promptly collapsed on the carpet, the perfect combination of tired and happy.

Bailey sent the boys upstairs to get ready for baths. While they complained verbally, they didn't hesitate to obey. She looked over at Nate. "Make yourself comfortable. We won't be long."

"Sounds good. I'll go out, grab a few things from my truck, and be right back."

He waited until they'd left, told Minnie to stay, and retrieved his large backpack that contained his clothes and personal hygiene items. Since he wasn't sure what to expect, he also brought in a sleeping bag and pillow. He didn't want to assume Bailey would have accommodations for him since all of this was last minute.

Nate got caught up on messages on his phone while he waited for Bailey and the boys to return. When they came back downstairs a half hour later, Seth and Jordan both had damp hair and were in their pajamas. Bailey had changed into a maroon T-shirt, and she must have twisted her hair into a new bun because the strands of hair that had escaped earlier were back in place.

She gave him an apologetic smile. "Let me get them a snack, and then we can get a space set up for you."

He followed the trio into the kitchen, where the boys took a seat at the small table tucked into the corner. "Anything I can do to help?"

"You can grab the jar of peanut butter out of the pantry." She pointed.

He found it easily and set it on the counter near where she was slicing apples. She added a generous swipe of peanut butter to each slice and set them in front of the boys. "As soon as you're done eating, we'll go brush teeth and get ready for bed."

Seth glanced at Nate and nodded. Jordan was too focused on his snack to respond at all.

Bailey leaned against the counter. There was no missing the exhaustion in her eyes.

Nate hoped and prayed that having backup at the house would help her relax enough to get a good night's sleep tonight.

Bailey stifled a yawn. "I figured Seth could sleep on the floor in my room so you can take his bed. I'll change the sheets quickly after I get them settled."

Nate immediately shook his head. "That's not necessary. Let Seth keep his room. I'd rather sleep down here in the living room." He was about to add where he could hear if anyone messed with either of the doors, but he didn't want the boys to worry about anything. "I brought a pillow and sleeping bag. The couch will be just fine."

She looked like she was going to argue, but Seth spoke up before she had the chance. "I could sleep in the living room, too. Like a sleepover!"

Jordan temporarily forgot about his snack and looked from his brother to his mom as though he were afraid that he was missing out on something.

"Absolutely not." Bailey gave her son a stern look. "You'll sleep in your own room like normal."

"Yes, ma'am." Seth went back to his snack, his disappointment written all over his face.

"Maybe we can play ball with Minnie some more tomorrow." Nate smiled when Seth's eyes brightened.

By half past eight, the boys were tucked in bed, and Bailey had finally given up convincing Nate that he ought to have something more comfortable to sleep on than the couch.

She'd brought out some peanut butter and chocolate candy, gotten each of them a soda, and now they were sitting in the living room. Bailey kicked off her shoes and rested her feet on the coffee table.

Nate chuckled. "You can tell a lot about a person when they prop their feet up like that."

Her eyebrows rose. "Oh?"

"It means you're laid back. More relaxed. I'll bet you don't have any of those fancy hand towels that are only for looks, do you?"

She was trying to keep a straight face, but one corner of her mouth quirked up.

"No fancy throw pillows either." He patted the arm of the couch.

"What makes you think Seth and Jordan haven't completely destroyed or hidden those by now?"

"Fair point. But I'm right about the hand towels, aren't I?"

Bailey shrugged her shoulders, but Nate could tell by the humor on her face that he'd hit the nail on the head.

"You're one of those people who isn't going to hang onto something or keep it around if it doesn't have some kind of practical purpose. It's not a bad trait, Bailey. I admire it."

"Thank you." A faint pink colored her cheeks. "I always figured it was a shame to have something and not actually use it. And for the record, we did have throw pillows with this couch, but they didn't last long around here." She took a bite of her candy and then gave a quiet moan of approval.

It was clear she savored the flavor, and her reaction was more than adorable. Was it candy in general? Chocolate? Or the combination of chocolate and peanut butter?

He suspected she saved the candy for herself in the evenings as a treat. Something to look forward to once the kids were in bed. If so, he appreciated the fact that she was willing to share.

They snacked in silence for several moments until Bailey took a drink of her soda before setting the can down on the coffee table. "You're good at reading people. Like, really good. I imagine Jenny and everyone else you worked with were sorry to see you go."

Her gray-blue eyes stayed on him as she waited for a response. When he said nothing, her brows furrowed a little. "Do you regret leaving the PD?"

Nate didn't want to talk about this or the reason for why he left the PD. All Bailey knew was that he'd decided to take some time and look into alternative work options. Few people truly understood the reasoning behind his decision. If they started this conversation, she'd eventually ask him for the details. Then, the answer would leave her as frustrated and disappointed with him as he was with himself.

He weighed his words carefully. "I don't regret it, but I do miss it. Especially everyone I worked with." He downed the rest of his soda. "I'd like to think I'm making a difference through Paws with a Cause, even if it's in a different way."

"Of course you are. I don't think that's ever been in question." She stared at her hands clasped in her lap and twiddled with the ring on her right index finger. "I just know you were great as a detective. Joe mentioned several times how you always wanted to help people and that you were one of the best detectives he'd ever known. I guess I never fully understood why you stepped away from that."

"It's complicated." The words came out with more of a growl than he'd intended. "I'm sorry, Bailey. It's not easy for me to talk about it."

"I understand. I'm sorry. I shouldn't have pried." With that, she stood and gathered their empty cans before going to the kitchen.

Nate could've kicked himself. She'd opened up yesterday about how conflicted she was concerning the farm. It couldn't have been easy to admit she was thinking about selling the place, and it was clear she had a lot of guilt over even entertaining the possibility. He wondered how many people she'd shared that with. Knowing how private a person she was, he doubted it was many, and she'd chosen to share with him.

Well, he hadn't talked about what happened to him with very many people, either. Maybe it was time he added one more to that list.

Chapter Fourteen

Bailey threw the soda cans away and stared at the trash can. Why had she asked Nate about leaving his job as a detective? Even when he left the police department a year and a half ago, he'd refused to say more than that he was taking time to re-evaluate his career. It wasn't long before he started working for Paws with a Cause, and then he never went back.

She suspected it had to do with a case. There'd been a couple of rough ones the month he left. Even Jenny didn't say much. Bailey figured she felt loyal to Nate, and Bailey couldn't blame her.

Movement at the kitchen door caught her attention. She looked up to find Nate leaning against the doorframe watching her.

"I'm sorry." He slipped his hands into his pockets. "I hate talking about it because it brings up a lot of memories that I wish I could just forget."

His voice was strong, but there was a flash of pain in his eyes.

Her heart hurt for him and whatever he went through.

"You don't need to feel obligated to talk to me—or anyone—about it."

"Thanks for that." He pushed away from the doorframe. "I'd still like to tell you if you're up to it. Please."

"Of course."

He shifted so that she could precede him into the living room. She caught a hint of his cologne as she passed him on her way back to the couch.

Nate joined her, rubbing the palms of his hands against his jeans. "Last February, I took on a case. A little girl had disappeared from her own backyard, and her parents were frantic to find her. Originally, we had no suspects. We started looking into the father's brother, who they didn't have a good relationship with. We canvassed the neighborhood and even spoke to her preschool teacher. At one point, we wondered if one of the parents was covering for the other." He crossed his arms. "When working a case, it's important to care about the people you're helping, but you have to maintain a level of distance so you can think objectively."

There was no doubt in her mind that this story didn't have a happy ending, and she steeled herself for the details. "But you couldn't keep that distance. Not this time."

He shook his head. "Her name was Lana, and there was something about her. She was four, had fiery red hair, and the greatest smile. Her favorite color was purple, she loved Minnie Mouse, and her favorite food was pancakes. Her parents said she lit up a room, and I have no doubt that's true. But I never got to meet her." A sad smile quickly fell away.

Bailey swallowed hard. She could picture Nate frantically searching for Lana, doing everything he could to find her.

"I couldn't eat. Couldn't sleep. The case consumed me." He swallowed hard. "We found her just over forty-eight hours after she disappeared, but it was too late. Evidence took us to the neighbor who lived next to Lana's family." Nate turned tortured eyes on her. "Bailey, I spoke to that man twice. *Twice.* And I had no idea. What kind of detective does that make me?"

"Oh, Nate. I can't even imagine..." Her throat ached as tears filled her eyes. "You couldn't have known. Not even her parents knew it was the neighbor. You did everything you could to find her."

"And it wasn't enough. I'll always wonder if, had I kept that distance, maybe I could've seen something in the guy when I'd interviewed him. Figured it out in time to get her back to her parents."

"Or maybe the monster who killed her knew exactly what to say to keep you—and the rest of the police—off his trail." Bailey curled one leg under the other and shifted on the couch so her body was turned toward him. "It wasn't your fault, Nate. Her murderer is the one responsible, and he doesn't deserve for you to take part of that blame." She reached across the space between them and laid her hand on his arm.

"I know you're right. Now. A couple of months later, I found out about a grief counseling group and stopped by on a whim. I really didn't think it'd help me. But being able to talk to other people who were dealing with the same emotional struggles that I was...it was cathartic. It took the rest of that year to start to heal. Most days are better, but sometimes, I still battle the guilt and anger. More often than I'd like. Adopting Minnie helped a lot, too."

He seemed focused on her hand. She should move it, but even as her brain registered the thought, it refused to pass the command along. Bailey looked from him to the dog, and suddenly, she understood where the name came from. "Her name…"

"I named her in honor of Lana because Minnie Mouse was her favorite."

More tears burned her eyes, and she blinked them away. "I'm sure Lana would've loved that. I'm glad the counseling helped. I really admire you for being willing to go through that and to find a way to get help when you needed it." His arm felt like it was hot enough to burn her palm. She finally pulled her hand away and tucked it under her knee. "Do you think you'll ever be able to go back to the police department? Do you think you'll even want to?"

Nate rubbed his arm where her hand had been a moment before. "Honestly? I don't know. I'm not sure I'll ever be ready."

"I remember the case, but I had no idea you…" She took in a steady breath. "I wish I could've done something to help you."

He shook his head. "There's nothing you could've done. I've had to work through it. And if there's one thing I've learned, there's no fast-tracking things when it comes to processing grief and guilt."

"Isn't that the truth." It'd been over two years since Joe died, and still, the grief crept in when she least expected it. She chuckled with a shake of her head. "We're quite the pair, aren't we?"

When she looked up at him, she found him studying her. A flash of something she didn't quite understand passed across his face.

Suddenly, Minnie sat up when she'd been asleep moments before. Her ears perked, and she looked in the direction of the front door. A low growl emanated from her chest as she continued to stare.

Nate got to his feet and reached for his gun. Minnie stood, her movement punctuated by a deep bark.

He glanced at Bailey and whispered, "Do you have your weapon?"

She nodded and stood as well. The weight of the gun nestled in the waist of her pants gave her some comfort. She didn't intend to take it off until she was getting ready for bed. "Do you think someone's out there?"

"I don't know, but I'm going to take a look and find out."

Chapter Fifteen

Bailey didn't like the idea of Nate going outside. What if someone else was out there, waiting for him in the dark? Would Minnie be able to tell in time to warn Nate? At the same time, if someone was snooping around the house, they had to put a stop to it.

"Please be careful."

"I will. Stay here, lock the door behind me, and don't open it again until you hear my voice on the other side." He waited long enough for her to meet his eyes and agree. He snapped a leash onto Minnie's collar, flipped the front porch light on, and exited the house.

She quickly locked the door again and resisted the urge to watch from one of the windows. She took in shallow breaths as she listened, hoping to get a hint of what might be happening outside. "God, please keep them safe," she prayed under her breath.

It wasn't five minutes later that a soft knock came on the door. "It's me, Bailey." She opened it, but he didn't come inside. "I don't see anything, and Minnie's relaxed again. I'm going to take a few minutes and walk her around the house. It might help her to get a sense of what's normal at night. Lock the door again, and we'll be back shortly."

"Okay." She did as he asked and tried to sit down, but that lasted mere seconds before she was on her feet again. She wiped off the kitchen counters and restocked the sodas in the fridge while she waited for him to return.

When he knocked on the door again, the sound made Bailey jump. She rolled her eyes at herself and waited to hear his voice before opening it. Nate came inside, holstered his weapon, and let his dog off the leash.

"There's no way to know for sure, but she most likely heard a small animal or something like that. If it was a person snooping around, then they had to have heard her bark. It's good for them to know she's here. That you and the boys aren't alone."

Now that he was safely back in the house, the fear and worry settled over her like a weight. Suddenly cold, she crossed her arms in front of her and swallowed hard.

What if this person didn't stop until she finally agreed to sell the place? What if they decided threats alone weren't enough? What if there was more than one person involved?

"Bailey?"

She blinked to find Nate standing directly in front of her, leaning down to study her face, his own filled with concern. "Sorry. I don't know why I'm reacting like this."

"Are you kidding? I'd be more worried if you weren't." He reached out and gently squeezed her arm. "We're going to figure out who's behind this. Come on, let's go sit back down and figure out a strategy." He led the way back to the living room, where he regained his spot on the couch.

She sat down again. "Strategy?"

"For getting the shop cleaned up. I figured I'd start first thing tomorrow by repairing the goat pen. That way, when

Poppy's well enough, you'll have a place to put them. After that, all you have to do is tell me what you need help with, and I'm there."

"Even if we work all day, I'm not sure we can get everything cleaned up and ready to open to the public by Friday."

"Then we get started and see where we end up. We aren't going to know until we try."

It was hard for her to imagine making the kind of progress they needed in time. But he was right; all they could do was try. And if he was willing to help, then they'd get a lot more done together than she ever could on her own.

Minnie wandered over and laid her head on his lap. Nate ran a thumb up the bridge of her nose and his hand over her head. She kept adoring eyes locked on his face.

Of course, she thought the world of him. Nate had taken her in when she had no home and shown her love. He was her hero.

Bailey hated that Lana's case had made him question so many things about himself and his career. Maybe he couldn't find Lana in time, but there were countless others that he'd helped. She'd be praying that he'd see the truth in that.

The jangle of the tags on Minnie's collar and the hum of the refrigerator were about the only sounds in the quiet house.

Bailey yawned and quickly covered her mouth with one hand. A glance at the clock surprised her. How was it already ten-thirty?

As if he'd read her mind, Nate gave Minnie a final pat and stood. "You should get some rest. I know you've mentioned that the boys are usually up early."

She wanted to object, but he was right. She was even

more tired than normal after not sleeping well the last few nights. "Yeah. I probably should. Are you sure you're okay with the sleeping bag and couch?"

"I wouldn't have said it if I didn't mean it." He gave her a kind smile. "Minnie and I will be just fine. Go and get a good night's sleep. We've got everything under control down here."

Nate had come over several times before Joe died, so he knew the layout of the house. Still, it didn't seem right to just leave him down here. But she knew him well enough to know there was no changing his mind. "All right. Please tell me if you need anything. Good night, Nate."

"Good night."

Bailey went upstairs to the master bedroom and closed the door behind her. As weird as it was to know that Nate was staying in the living room, it also put her mind at ease. There was some guilt that he might not sleep well, but the thought of being able to rest without worrying about someone messing with the house took a huge weight off her shoulders.

She took a quick shower, blow-dried her hair, and then fell asleep moments after her head hit the pillow.

For the first time in months, she had a dream about Joe. In the past, they either involved his accident and the night-mare surrounding it, or it would be a replay of something they'd done together as a family: the birth of one of the boys, a camping trip, or a special Christmas memory. She'd had one of those dreams nearly every night for a long time, but recently they'd started to dwindle.

This one was different. In her dream, she awakened to find Joe standing beside the bed, a sweet smile on his face. He looked down at her with such love that her heart nearly burst. He never said a word as he softly brushed some hair from her forehead and leaned over to kiss her there.

He gave her hand a squeeze and then turned, walking out of the room and closing the door behind him. In the dream, Bailey knew he was leaving for good—that she'd never see him again—but she had peace about it.

She woke up with a start, momentarily disoriented. She pressed a hand to the spot on her forehead where Joe had kissed her and tried to separate her own feelings from those she'd experienced in the dream. There was still a sadness there, but it was as though it were blanketed with a layer of peace that had the quieting effect of snowfall on the chaotic world.

It was only then that she realized her cheeks were wet with tears. She dried them with a corner of her sheet and was about to lie down and try to get more sleep when Seth's screams made her jump out of bed and almost out of her skin.

"Mommy! Help me!"

Chapter Sixteen

After bidding Bailey good night, Nate got the couch set up. He opted to sleep in his jeans and T-shirt in case he had to get up quickly in the night, but he did empty the contents of his pockets into a zippered section of his backpack so he'd be more comfortable.

He'd also brought a small gun safe that only opened in response to his fingerprints. That way he had a safe place to put his handgun while he was sleeping. He didn't know if Seth and Jordan ever wandered downstairs at night or not, but he didn't want to risk it.

Even though his body was tired, his mind was much too busy to fall asleep. He double-checked that all the doors and windows on the bottom floor were closed and locked. After that, he pulled up the Bible app on his phone and spent some time reading the book of John. The last thing he did before falling asleep was to pray for Bailey, Seth, and Jordan. "And Lord, please give everyone wisdom. Help us figure out who's doing this to Bailey, and give me the ability to keep her and the boys safe."

He uttered a quiet "amen" before falling asleep.

It was Minnie who woke him up an hour later. She didn't bark, but she did get to her feet and pace past the coffee table, her eyes alert.

Nate sat up and quickly opened the gun safe. "What is it, girl?" He waited silently, listening to the unfamiliar creaks of the house and hoping to pick up anything that didn't belong. Minnie cocked her head to one side and looked upward. Was someone moving around upstairs that she could hear but he couldn't quite detect?

He was just about to relax again when Seth's frantic voice carried from upstairs, "Mommy! Help me!"

Minnie woofed, and Nate leaped to his feet. He grabbed his handgun and secured it on his belt before taking the stairs two at a time. At the top, he spotted Seth's bedroom door open and the light on down the hall. He told Minnie to stay and crept closer. Right outside the room, he heard Bailey's voice as she tried to console her son.

"It was just a dream, sweetie. I promise. Everything's okay."

A little whimper was followed by sniffles. "He opened my window and came in. He was really scary."

"Let me tell you something. No one is coming in your window. For one thing, they'd have to scale the side of our house like Spider-Man to get to it. Do you really think someone could do that?"

Nate imagined the little boy shaking his head no, tears in his dark eyes.

"Of course not! Plus, we have locks on all the windows. They can't be opened from the outside."

"What about downstairs? The bad guy can reach the windows."

It was hard for Nate not to go in and try to reassure the

little boy himself. Instead, he continued to listen, impressed by how well Bailey seemed to be handling the situation. Her voice was soft and soothing. He imagined her sitting on the edge of the bed, smoothing back Seth's hair or holding his hand.

"The windows downstairs all have locks. The same with the doors. Plus, Nate and Minnie are sleeping down there. If someone tried to come into the house, Minnie would know it before they ever stepped foot inside. Can you imagine being a bad guy and sneaking into the house only to find a big dog like Minnie waiting for you?"

The two of them giggled together, and the sound warmed Nate's heart. If his presence there at the house today only served to make Seth feel safer after a bad dream, then it was all worth it.

"Will you sing me a song? Please?"

"One song, and then you'd better get some sleep. You need to make more energy so you can play with Minnie tomorrow. She'll be disappointed if you're too tired to play ball with her."

Seth must have agreed because a moment later, Bailey's sweet, soft voice filled the air as she began to sing a lullaby.

Had Nate ever heard her sing before? Maybe with a group at a birthday party, but not like this. He suddenly felt like he was intruding and considered trying to retreat downstairs when Bailey spoke again.

"Sleep well, my boy. I'll see you in the morning."

"Night, Mommy."

"I love you."

"I love you, too."

With that, Bailey backed into the hallway and quietly closed Seth's bedroom door. She turned, spotted him, and didn't seem the least bit surprised that he was there.

Nate, on the other hand, took in the way her dark blonde hair cascaded in waves past her shoulders to the middle of her back. His hand itched to reach out and see if it was as soft and thick as it looked.

It didn't matter that she was standing there in a pair of loose pajama pants and an oversized sweatshirt. Beautiful didn't even begin to describe her.

His throat went dry, and he swallowed hard. "I'm sorry to intrude. I heard him cry out and came up to make sure everything was okay."

She nodded and motioned for him to follow her to the top of the stairs so they were farther away from Seth's room. "I appreciate it. I guess the break-in at the store and everything else has bothered him more than I realized." She crossed her arms in front of her and frowned. "I wish I'd known—I would've done more to reassure him."

"You were great in there, Bailey. They're lucky to have you for their mom."

"Thank you." She blinked several times and then reached a hand down to pat Minnie. "Maybe, when this is all over, I'll seriously consider getting a dog. Just knowing you and Minnie were downstairs made Seth feel better."

"Dogs have a way of doing that." Nate scratched Minnie's ear, and his hand brushed against Bailey's.

She didn't immediately move hers away. "Dogs and their stubborn owners."

There was just enough light in the hallway for him to make out the humor that sparked in her eyes. It took everything in him not to reach for her hand, but if he did that, he wasn't sure he could stop himself from kissing her.

Nate shifted his position and shoved his hands deep into his pockets. "I'm glad we can help. Do you think you'll be able to go back to sleep?"

Bailey pulled the ends of her sleeves down to cover her fingers. "I think so. You?"

"We'll be fine. See you in the morning."

She nodded, and Nate made himself turn and go back downstairs. One thing was certain: the image of Bailey standing in the dim light, her hair flowing around her shoulders, was something he'd never forget.

Chapter Seventeen

The rest of the night passed without incident. Nate never heard either of the boys wake up again, and if Bailey had trouble sleeping, he couldn't tell. He started the day at just before six o'clock feeling rested. Hopefully, they'd make some good headway with clean-up and repairs. With any luck, Jenny or someone else from the police department would contact them with an update.

He got ready for the day. It wasn't long before thumps and shifting upstairs let him know that everyone else was waking up. From the sound of it, the boys jumped into the day with as much enthusiasm as they tackled everything else.

Both boys stomped down the stairs, closely followed by Bailey. She'd dressed in a pair of faded blue jeans and a blue T-shirt that brought out the color of her eyes. She'd also pulled her hair up into a bun again, and Nate had to ignore the pang of disappointment at not having the opportunity to see it loose in the daylight.

He focused on the boys as they ran straight over to lavish Minnie with attention.

He chuckled. "I see where I rate." He ran a hand over his short goatee and mustache. "It's got to be all her fur. Maybe if I grow the facial hair out a little more, I might have a chance of competing..."

Bailey gave an adorable snort and slapped a hand over her mouth.

Suddenly, he wanted to know what she thought about his goatee and mustache. Did she approve? It shouldn't even matter to him, but he couldn't deny that it did. "When I first grew a mustache and goatee in high school, my mom hated it. She said it made me look too old. Unfortunately for her, my dad liked it, and she was outvoted. I've kept it ever since."

"I think the look suits you." She cleared her throat and tried to corral the boys. "Come on, guys. Go sit down at the table."

At that moment, Nate was glad he'd listened to his dad instead of his mom.

He followed the family into the kitchen. Seth and Jordan climbed into chairs around the table while Bailey got out several boxes of cereal, milk, orange juice, and set a stack of bowls and four spoons on the table.

She flashed Nate an apologetic look. "I'm sorry. Mondays are cereal mornings."

"Are you kidding? I like cereal as much as the next person." He took Minnie out to do her business and then got her some food before joining the family at the table. It was nice to be a part of their lives during such a normal part of the day.

From that point on, the day flew by. He helped them check on Poppy's wounds and take care of the rest of the animals. Then he made sure the store was secure before dropping Bailey off there with Jordan. He would've offered to take the younger boy to work on the goat pen, but he was worried Jordan would wander off or get himself into trouble. This way, he and Seth could get the pen repaired as fast as possible and get back to help.

Seth seemed to soak up the attention and instruction. Nate truly enjoyed having the boy there with him. Together, they replaced the gate and repaired any fencing around the pen that had been damaged. By the time they were done, the pen was ready for the goats as soon as Poppy was healed up.

"What do you think?" Nate placed a hand on the boy's shoulder.

"It looks awesome." Seth turned and looked up, his expression hopeful. "I think we make a good team. Don't you?"

"Absolutely. I'd work with you again anytime." He gave the boy a fist bump.

It saddened Nate to think that Joe was missing out on these moments with his son. As long as he had Bailey's blessing, he planned to keep spending time with Seth and Jordan, make sure to be there for them, and remind them of how much their father loved them.

"Come on, let's get back to the store and help your mom."

❋

Nate and Bailey sorted through merchandise for four hours. She was skilled at giving Seth little jobs to keep him busy while doing her best to keep Jordan from getting into things. The latter was a lot easier said than done. Nate knew he was curious and busy but didn't realize how much he kept Bailey on her toes.

She kept a running list of products that were damaged or destroyed so she could submit a thorough inventory to the insurance company. Meanwhile, Nate and Seth would bag items for the garbage.

Nate had left Minnie at the house. There was a lot of food-related merchandise scattered on the floor. He couldn't trust her not to sample her way through the store.

Nate and Bailey's phones both pinged with an incoming text.

He glanced at his screen. "It's from Jenny. She's at the gate and coming in."

Bailey looked up from a pile of papers that she'd stacked on the main counter. "I wonder why she's stopping by." She blew a wayward strand of hair out of her face.

Nate gave Seth a lighter bag of trash to carry, and they took several out to the dumpster behind the store. By the time they got back, Jenny's police car was pulling up in front. She got out and waved at Seth with a smile. "Hey, kiddo!"

He gave her a happy wave. "We've been working hard all day! Are you here to see?"

"Most definitely."

The three of them went back into the store. Nate frowned because, despite all their hard work, it barely looked like they'd touched the mess. Bailey might have been right when she originally said she wasn't sure she could have things cleaned up in time to open on Friday.

Jenny walked over and gave Bailey a hug. "Hey, looks like you've been busy."

"Very. Although we haven't lost as much as I first thought we had. Which is good." She shrugged. "But it's going to be time-consuming to sort through it all."

"I can imagine. Well, I don't have much news, but I had

Detective Paris's blessing to come and give you a quick update on the case."

Bailey glanced at Jordan to make sure he was still busy with the blocks he was playing with and then leaned against the counter. "Any luck at all with identifying who did this?"

After opening a notes app on her phone, Jenny gave a shake of her head. "Not yet. The for sale sign is one that could be purchased from a number of places in town, or it could've been one someone held onto for a while. No usable prints. None. It must've been wiped down before it was placed because there would have at least been prints from the store where it was purchased."

Nate wasn't surprised, but he hated to see the disappointment on Bailey's face.

She frowned. "I was really hoping there'd be something they could use."

"I know. Me, too." Jenny gave her friend a sympathetic look. "Officers walked your property line. All the fencing looks great. There's no damage or obvious point of entry. Right now, we're going through all the evidence collected from here, but as you know, it's going to be hard to find much. I did want to mention that you should look for anything out of place while you're cleaning up just in case our suspect left something behind. This is a lot of damage in a relatively short period of time. It would be easy to drop an item or even lose a button or something like that."

"Makes sense." Bailey hiked an eyebrow. "Not that I'm not happy to see you, but you could've told me all of this over the phone. Why did you drive all the way out here?"

"Because I took a long lunch break, thought I'd bring chicken strips and fries to share, and then figured I could pitch in for half an hour or so before I head back." She grinned when her mention of food snagged the boys' attention. "Seth, will you help me bring lunch in please?"

While they went to get lunch from Jenny's car, Nate moved to stand beside Bailey. "I can run into town this afternoon and get some cameras. We can set one up at the main gate and another at the front of the store. At least if anyone else tries to put up another sale sign or break into the store, we'll have it recorded."

"That would be great. Thank you."

He intended to buy a third one to cover the front door of her house, too. If it were up to him, he'd get an alarm system installed. He knew it wasn't something Bailey would be open to. In that case, Nate had every intention of sticking around until they caught whoever was behind this.

Chapter Eighteen

I t was nice to have Jenny stay for lunch and to help with cleanup for a little while. There was still so much to get done, and for Bailey, it was a constant struggle to keep from getting frustrated or overwhelmed. It truly made a difference, however, to have two of her friends there to keep conversation going and to make her laugh. Oh, they were both in rare form. Bailey didn't think she'd laughed that much in a long time.

When it was time for Jenny to get back to work, she left but returned minutes later.

Bailey jogged out to her squad car. "Did you forget something?"

"This was taped to your mailbox." Jenny handed a piece of paper over, a hopeful look on her face.

Bailey took one of the flyers she'd printed out about the lost goats. At the bottom was a note that said, "I think one of your goats wandered onto my property. Drop by anytime. We're keeping her safe."

Below that was a name, Fred Anson, and an address and phone number.

Bailey shook her head in wonder. "Wouldn't that be something if Petunia were still alive? Oh, the boys would be so relieved. What are the odds that it's someone else's miniature goat?"

"Probably not good," Jenny said with a chuckle. "I hope it works out. Make sure Nate goes with you, okay? Let me know."

"Will do. Thanks again."

Back inside the store, she showed the flyer to Nate. "Do you mind if we take a break and head over there? If it *is* Petunia, it'd be good to make sure she's okay before the vet's office closes."

"Sure, not a problem." He dusted his hands off on his pants. "Do you know Fred Anson?"

"Not really. I think we met them right after we bought this place, but we never really chatted."

"So he's never expressed an interest in buying your land?"

She blinked at him in surprise. "No, not that Joe ever mentioned. I hadn't even thought about a neighbor being behind all of this."

"I'm just looking at options. I can see someone wanting to buy adjacent land to expand what they own, especially if they have significant mineral rights. It'd be easy to get onto your property and back home in the middle of the night, too."

Bailey had a hard time accepting the possibility. "So you're thinking that Fred could've vandalized the goat pen and taken Petunia to his property himself?"

"I'm saying it's a possibility. I'm going to call the station and have them run a background check on him. See if anything pops up. Then we can go over and see if the goat he found is Petunia."

"That sounds good."

Nate dialed a number on his phone. "Hey, Logan, I need you to run a background check on someone…" He walked to the back of the store until Bailey couldn't hear what he was saying anymore.

Seth was practically hopping up and down in excitement. "Oh, I hope it's Petunia! I'll bet the other goats will be so happy to see her again!"

She knelt at his level. "You need to remember that the man may be mistaken. It could be that he's found a different goat. We won't know until we get there."

"But I can hope. My teacher at church says it's always important to have hope."

His simple faith and positivity brought a smile to Bailey's face. "Yes, we can always have hope." She ruffled his hair.

While she waited for Nate to finish his phone call, she called Fred to make sure he was home and that it was okay to swing by. She'd just ended the conversation when Nate walked up.

"I spoke to a friend in the IT department. Nothing jumped out about your neighbor—no criminal record. Aside from a couple of parking tickets, his record is clean. It seems like a big leap to go from that to vandalism and issuing threats."

It did seem far-fetched. Then again, a few days ago, she'd never have imagined someone would be targeting her family like this at all.

They put a large crate in the back of Bailey's pickup truck, and Nate offered to drive it over to the Anson's place. The gate was open at the entrance, and a man was waiting on a four-wheeler. He lifted a hand in greeting and stepped down.

Bailey turned to look at the backseat. "You boys stay here. We'll be right back."

"It's good to see you again." Fred greeted her with a kind smile and shook her hand. The skin on his palm and fingers was covered in callouses. Judging from that and the well-used four-wheeler, he probably did a lot of hands-on work. "It's been a while. I was sorry to hear about your husband."

"Thank you." Bailey swallowed past the lump in her throat. "This is Nate Walker, a family friend." She waited for the men to shake hands before she continued. "I can't believe you might have found our missing goat. My sons have been so worried about her."

"You can imagine our surprise when my wife found her eating the bushes in her rose garden." He laughed with a shake of his head. "If you all want to follow me, I'll lead you to the shop around back. I really hope she's yours. I can't imagine too many miniature goats running around."

With that, Fred got back onto his four-wheeler and waited for them to rejoin the boys in the truck. They followed him past the house and garage and around the corner. A building that looked like a large shed came into view and there, in a small pen beside it, stood Petunia.

"It's her!" The triumphant cry came from Seth shortly followed by a joyful shout from Jordan.

Bailey breathed a sigh of relief. "Praise God." Not just because the goat was safe but because her boys no longer had to worry about their pet.

They piled out of the truck, and as soon as Petunia spotted them, she let out a series of long bleats.

Fred laughed loudly. "I guess that answers that question. I'm really glad you called me so quickly. I'm not sure that pen was going to hold her for long."

The three adults watched as the boys ran to the goat and petted her through the slats in the fencing. Bailey had no doubt Fred was right. Petunia could get out of that pen anytime she wanted to.

"Thank you so much, Mr. Anson, for taking the time to keep her safe and let us know you'd found her."

"Not a problem at all. I'm happy to help. My wife went by your store the other day for sunflowers and mentioned the flyers you'd handed out. I'm just glad we found her."

Bailey was about to call the boys over again when Nate lightly touched the small of her back before speaking.

"Mr. Anson, has anyone asked you about selling your property recently? Or asked you questions regarding Thompson Family Farm?"

"I get an inquiry or two every year asking if we're interested in selling." He shrugged. "There's no doubt someone could buy this place, split it into lots with new homes, and make a fortune. But Ginny and I aren't interested in that. We raised our kids here and enjoy having enough room for them to stay with the grandkids when they visit. You know what I mean?"

"Absolutely." Nate gave him a nod. "Can't say I blame you. And no one has asked you about the Thompson farm?"

"Not a soul." Fred looked over at the boys who were still lavishing the goat with praise and pats. "Your sons remind me of my own kids when they were that age. Time sure does fly by. I have grandkids not much older than them now."

"It sure does." Bailey couldn't believe how much her boys had grown and changed over the last year or two. "Thank you again for taking care of Petunia. We'll get her loaded into the truck and out of your hair."

She hadn't really thought Mr. Anson was behind everything, but as soon as they'd spoken to him, she knew there was no way he was responsible. In some ways, it would've been easier if he had been.

Someone out there was determined to force Bailey to sell her home or destroy her business in the process. She prayed that they'd get a breakthrough in the case before things got worse.

Chapter Nineteen

Nate sat at Bailey's kitchen table with both his phone and hers in front of him. He'd purchased three cameras and placed them at the main gate, the store entrance, and the front door of the house.

He'd expected Bailey to object to that last one, but she didn't, which told Nate just how much all of this had shaken her.

Now, he was trying to connect the feeds to an app that would allow them to view the cameras from anywhere. Bailey said it was fine for him to add the app to his phone, and he promised her he would delete it once everything got sorted out.

She wandered into the living room, where the boys were playing with Minnie and being overly energetic. It was no wonder—they'd been cooped up in the store most of the day. "Hey, guys. I need you to tone it down before someone gets hurt."

The boys agreed, but their energy levels didn't come down much.

Nate gave a nod of satisfaction when the three feeds

finally loaded on Bailey's phone. "I've got the cameras linked. Do you want me to show you how this works?"

She took a chair at the small table and scooted it next to his so she could see the screen more easily. Her shoulder brushed his briefly, and he did his best to ignore the scent of her shampoo or whatever it was that had her smelling like something soft and floral.

He explained how to view all three feeds together, how to enlarge each one, and then how to look up past instances of activity that would be recorded from now on.

"It should only record human activity. I told it to ignore animals; otherwise, you'd get an activity report for every bird or squirrel that moves on screen."

Bailey accepted the phone from him and touched the feed showing the front gate. "This is great. Thank you."

"You're welcome." He studied her for a moment. "I hate to ask this, but have you had any family members or friends express an interest in your business or land?"

She looked up from her phone, clearly surprised by the question. "No one. It was clear that Joe's parents didn't approve of our decision to take most of our savings and put it into this place. Plus, Joe liked to talk about retiring to run it together at some point. His dad worked as a police officer his whole life, and I don't think he could understand how Joe would be willing to walk away from it. If anyone else objected or wanted the land, they sure didn't tell us."

Nate remembered Joe talking about his father and how difficult he'd been when they first made the decision to buy the land. Joe hadn't understood why his father was so against it when he had followed in his father's footsteps already. Afterward, he'd promised that he would support his own sons in their occupational choices no matter what.

If Nate were to be blessed with children in the future, he'd feel the same way.

"What about competition? Is there any place in town or nearby that has a similar business setup? Someplace that you have to worry about taking customers away from you or vice versa?"

"Not really. Most of the local farms sell their produce or other products at the Farmer's Market downtown. I even stock some of their things in my store, like soap, honey, and salsa. I figure people who come here are going to be more interested in purchasing items that are made and grown locally. I can't imagine anyone who would try to put me out of business."

Bailey crossed her arms and rested them on the table. "And if Joe's parents had wanted to sabotage the farm to prevent us from turning it into a business, surely they would've done that from the start and not waited until now."

"I tend to agree with you."

The sound of thuds approached from the living room as Seth and Jordan ran into the kitchen closely followed by Minnie.

"We're bored." Seth folded his arms in front of him, the exact same stance as his mom when she was determined to do something.

Nate hid a smile.

Jordan nodded. "I'm bored."

Poor Bailey looked exhausted as she glanced at the watch on her left wrist. "What about a walk? Then we'll get home in time to make dinner. How does that sound?"

"Yes!" With that, Jordan ran to the banister and disappeared upstairs.

Seth's face brightened. "Can we go on the haunted trail? Please? It's been forever."

Haunted Trail? Nate had no idea what that was.

"Go upstairs and get your shoes and socks on. Then we'll talk about where we're going to walk."

"Okay. Thanks, Mom!"

Nate told Minnie to sit so she didn't follow Seth upstairs. The poor dog clearly didn't like being left behind. "So what's the haunted trail?"

"It's what Joe called the trail that leads from our house to the old barn. He told spooky stories the first time he took Seth, and it made a big impression. I haven't been out that way in a while." She didn't look sold on the idea. "Seth's always found the old barn fascinating, which is why it makes me nervous. There's no telling how sound the structure is."

"I think Joe might have shown me the barn when he brought me by not long after you guys bought the place, but I haven't seen it since. If you're going to be contacting companies in the next week or two to see about having it leveled, it won't hurt to have pictures to send. I'm good with it if that's what you guys want to do. Or I can go another time and take pictures for you."

Bailey glanced at the staircase. Judging by the frantic stomping upstairs, the boys were getting ready and would be back down any minute. "It'd be good for them to get some exercise, and you're right. I should get some pictures in case I need them." A smile tugged at the corners of her mouth. "Besides, we desperately need some rain. Going for a long walk without umbrellas practically guarantees that'll happen."

Twenty minutes later, they set out along a narrow trail that led away from the Thompson's backyard and to the northeast. It didn't take long for Seth and Jordan to find walking sticks as they led the way. Bailey and Nate walked side by side behind them. Minnie, who was on a long leash, happily trotted along, her nose to the ground.

"It really is pretty out here," Nate commented as he took in the trees around them. He'd traveled to different areas of the United States in the past, but the Texas Hill Country was still his favorite place.

He glanced at Bailey, relieved to see that some of the tension in her shoulders seemed to ease as they walked. Apparently, she needed to get out and away from everything herself.

The path—if it was even wide enough to be considered one—was so narrow that walking beside Bailey meant touching shoulders on occasion. More than once, their hands brushed against each other. Nate imagined a situation where he could hold her hand, and she'd lean against him to laugh at something silly the boys did. The thought sent warmth through his chest.

Had she and Joe done that very thing while walking this same path? The question sobered him. Suddenly, the air felt heavy, and Nate wasn't sure if it was from the weight of memories or if it was because the humidity had increased when the clouds rolled in. Most likely, it was a combination. For the first time since he'd arrived at the house to stay for a few days, Nate felt like he was intruding.

"We're almost there!" Seth announced loudly and picked up some speed. Jordan struggled to keep up with his big brother.

Bailey raised her voice. "When you see the barn, stop and wait for us. Do not go to the barn."

"Yes, ma'am." The little boys' voices sounded out in unison.

Nate shoved his melancholy thoughts aside and focused on the building that appeared in the clearing. He wasn't sure what he'd expected. Maybe something around the size of the small barn that Bailey used now.

This was so much larger, and Bailey wasn't exaggerating when she said it was rundown. No wonder Joe referred to it as haunted. It would be the perfect location for a horror movie.

He took in the sagging roof, the siding that at one time was probably red was now covered in mold and cracking due to exposure to the elements. Even the large barn doors were tilted off their tracks. He doubted anyone had used the building in decades.

"It's so cool," Seth said in awe. "Like right out of an adventure story."

"Wow!" Jordan stared at it. "It's broken."

His simple description made Bailey chuckle. "Yes, it is. Very broken. And dangerous. There's a good chance part of the ceiling or walls could fall at any minute." She waited until they were both looking at her. "That's why it's important that you never, ever go inside. Do you understand?"

The boys nodded, their faces serious.

There were piles of stones that made a border of sorts. Bailey told them they could play there if they wanted to. Now, the boys were jumping from stone to stone and trying not to touch the ground. Minnie whined, but Nate refused to let her off the leash. She generally behaved well, but the last thing he wanted her to do was to run into the barn.

"I can see why you want to tear it down. You can't have people coming onto your property and wandering around here." He glanced at her profile. She was looking at the barn with a critical eye. "What are you picturing?"

· "This is the perfect location for another pumpkin patch.

With all the trees around it, it'd be a fun place to take people on a hayride for them to choose a pumpkin of their own. Don't you think?" Bailey turned her head to look at him.

"Yeah, I think it'd be perfect." But even with his reassurance, she seemed reluctant. "What's wrong?"

She folded her arms in front of her and shivered. "This place gives me the creeps. I can't explain why. It always has, though. Maybe it's just the ambiance of it and the fact that it was abandoned here to rot."

Right on cue, something inside the barn cracked loud enough to draw the attention of the little boys. They stopped jumping and turned to look at the building, their eyes wide.

"That's exactly why you should listen to your mom and never go inside that building," Nate told them, his voice serious and louder than necessary. He understood why Bailey was worried because it was clear that Seth, especially, found the place fascinating.

Thunder rumbled in the distance, drawing Nate's attention to the sky. The white cloud coverage had turned to a dull gray. A wall of black clouds on the horizon promised rain and potentially more severe weather ahead. "You'd better get your pictures so we can head back before that storm gets here."

Chapter Twenty

Bailey looked up at the sky. This had the potential to be the first bad thunderstorm of the season. Yes, it was time to get back home. She watched as Nate walked over and helped Jordan down from the tall rock he was balanced on.

"Lead the way, Seth," Bailey instructed, knowing full well her son would be happy to take on the challenge.

He scrambled to the ground, picked up his walking stick, and started back the way they'd come. "Come on, Jordan. Let's go!"

What began as a light rain quickly turned to a downpour minutes later. Even the boys, who'd originally laughed and splashed in the puddles, looked like half-drowned puppies. Minnie kept her head down, ears tucked close, and trotted down the path as quickly as Nate would allow her.

At first, Bailey had tried to use her arms to keep the rain off her face. There was no use anymore, though. The weight of her wet hair caused it to fall out of its bun. Cold strands of hair clung to her cheeks.

She laughed. "Well, they wanted an adventure."

Nate looked over at her, humor in his dark eyes. "I like that you're not annoyed by this."

"Why be upset? We desperately needed rain. Seth will probably remember this forever, and it's been a welcome break from everything else that's been going on."

Her shoe hit a slick spot. She gasped as she lost her balance. Nate's arm shot out and wrapped around her waist, halting her fall.

"Are you okay?" His warm breath brushed against her cheek as he slowly released her, moving his grasp to her hand. Minnie walked over and licked her free one in concern.

Thankfully, Seth and Jordan stopped ahead to wait for them.

"I'm good. Thank you for that." Bailey took a step forward and nearly slipped again. She tightened her grip on his hand to keep her balance as she picked her way through the muddy spot to the rockier part of the path.

The cool rain had effectively chilled her to the core. The only part of her that didn't feel cold was the hand that Nate continued to hold in his. The sensation sent butterflies zigzagging in her stomach, which immediately brought feelings of confusion and guilt. She didn't know what to make of her recent attraction toward Nate. All she knew was that a part of her hoped he wouldn't let go.

Except she was being ridiculous. He was simply trying to give her extra stability as they hurried back to her house, nothing more. Which meant her reaction to it made no sense whatsoever.

Her cheeks warmed, and she was thankful for the cold rain that continued to pelt her face.

As soon as they climbed the steps to the covered porch

at the front of her house, Nate released her hand. She unlocked the door.

Nate shook his arms and ran a hand through his short hair. "Minnie is a muddy mess. I'll sit out here with her while you take care of the boys. Then, if you'll bring me an old towel, I'll get her cleaned up before we come inside."

Bailey told the boys to wait on the mat just inside the house and turned to look at Nate. "Aren't you freezing? It'll take me a few minutes to get this under control."

"I'm good. Truly. It's not nearly as cold now that we're out of the rain." He gave her an encouraging smile and tipped his head toward the door. "Go get the boys into some dry clothes."

"Okay. I'll be right back." Man, she hated to leave him standing out there. It might not be as bad now that he was out of the rain, but if he was even half as chilled as she was, he had to be miserable. "Take your shoes off here, guys, and then we'll go upstairs and change into some warm pajamas."

Seth managed his own clothes in the bathroom while Bailey helped Jordan get out of his wet clothing and into his pajamas. "When you two are done, I want you to play up here until I come get you. Then I'll make us some soup and grilled cheese sandwiches."

Both of her sons whooped with excitement, bringing a smile to her face.

She grabbed several towels from the bathroom and hurried downstairs. She stepped onto the porch just in time to catch droplets of water as Minnie shook herself.

"I'm so sorry." Nate reached for a towel and began to rub it up and down the dog's body. "I may have to carry her into the bathroom and wash the mud off, but at least I can keep her from dripping across your floor on the way in."

"It's fine. I don't think that's going to make my clothes

any wetter." Bailey chuckled as Minnie started to rub her sides against the towel in Nate's hand. "She's too smart for her own good."

"That she is." Nate stood and stepped on Minnie's leash while he grabbed for another towel, but instead of using it to dry his own hair, he wrapped it around Bailey's shoulders. "You're shivering."

Was she? Now that he mentioned it, she sure was, but she hadn't even noticed until then. She gathered the two corners of the towel together in one hand below her chin.

"Thank you." The words were barely above a whisper.

Nate gathered some of the wet hair that was pressed against her cheek and gently swept it behind her ear. "You're welcome." His voice sounded deeper than normal.

Instead of dropping his hand, it slipped into the hair at the base of her neck until he was cupping the back of her head.

Bailey's heart caught in her throat as her pulse thundered in her ears. The sound of Minnie shaking herself and the falling rain faded away. The porch light illuminated his dark eyes, and there was no missing the interest there that mingled with uncertainty.

As though it had a mind of its own, her free hand rested against his chest. She felt his heart racing beneath her palm through his rain-soaked shirt.

In a single motion, Nate dipped his head and touched his lips to hers in a whisper of a kiss. The sensations made her head spin. She grasped his shirt to keep herself grounded and leaned into him as she lifted her chin. He drew her closer, kissing her again, this time with an intensity that took her breath away.

The reality of what was happening crashed into her,

and her heart twisted painfully in her chest. She abruptly stepped away from him and inhaled with a gasp.

"Bailey, I—" His face morphed into a combination of fear and worry, but it was the flash of regret that caused confusion to course through her veins.

He reached out for her, but she shook her head.

"I need to check on the boys. Make sure they got dressed and that their muddy things aren't soaking into the carpet." She took several steps backward and hit the doorframe with her heel. "The downstairs bathroom is all yours. Soap and more towels are in the cabinet under the sink." Her own words sounded foreign to her ears, as though she were listening to them echo back from the other end of a long hallway.

With that, she turned and escaped into the house, swallowing back a sob.

Chapter Twenty-One

With a low growl, Nate slammed the palm of his hand against the porch railing. Eight years. He'd managed to hide how he felt about Bailey for eight years. Then he let his guard down for ten seconds and ruined everything. He was certain he'd seen the glitter of tears in her eyes before she'd run back into the house. He'd caused them, and he couldn't blame her if she hated him right now.

"I'm sorry, Joe. Please forgive me," he groaned.

He spotted a folded towel on the porch which she must have dropped before retreating inside. He picked that up, draped it over Minnie, and lifted her into his arms.

Awkwardly, he got her inside and closed and locked the door behind him. He left his shoes by the door before lugging the dog into the downstairs bathroom.

He was filling the bathtub with enough water to wash away the mud when a light tapping came from the door. Bailey's voice filtered through. "Nate? I set your duffel bag right outside."

"Thank you."

He waited a few moments before opening the door and bringing the bag inside.

It took more than twenty minutes to bathe Minnie and then take a shower himself after half of her mud ended up all over him. Now that her fur had been toweled dry and he was dressed in some fresh clothes himself, he opened the door and let the dog out.

He left the wet items in the bathtub with the intention of putting them in the washing machine as soon as space was available.

Voices filtered down the hall from the kitchen. He had no idea what to expect from Bailey, and the uncertainty had his stomach in knots.

He entered the kitchen and was immediately greeted by Seth. "Hey, Nate! Mom's making hot chocolate. Do you want some?"

Bailey was getting mugs from an overhead cabinet and placing them on the counter. She didn't turn around but said over her shoulder, "We've got plenty. While we're drinking that, I thought sandwiches and some soup would hit the spot for dinner."

"That sounds delicious. Thank you." He took a seat at the table and smiled at the boys. "You two look nice and warm in your pajamas. Did the rain count as your shower, or will you have to take a bath later?"

Seth wrinkled his nose. "We always have to take a bath."

Jordan simply shrugged.

Nate's gaze swung to Bailey as she spooned hot cocoa mix into each of the mugs. Instead of putting her hair in a bun, she'd braided it down her back, the ends still damp.

Instantly, the memory of how it felt to hold her in his arms and thread his fingers through her hair came to mind. He inhaled slowly and tried to shove the image away.

"Is there anything I can do to help?" His voice sounded loud in the unusually quiet kitchen.

"Could you get the marshmallows from the pantry? Top shelf on the right."

He found them easily and set them on the counter. She gave him a nod of thanks, but she'd yet to look at him since he came into the room. The tension was thicker than the dark liquid she was stirring in each mug.

She plopped two marshmallows in each of two mugs, added some milk to cool the liquid, and carried them over to the table. She set them in front of the boys and handed them spoons. "They're still really warm, so be careful."

Each of her sons spooned some liquid, blew on it, and then slurped with satisfaction.

When Bailey turned away from the table, she finally lifted her gaze to him. Immediately, her cheeks turned pink. "Do you like marshmallows in your hot chocolate?"

"Yes, please. Doesn't everyone?" He smiled, hoping their simple conversation might put her at ease.

"Well, they ought to." She added three marshmallows to each of their mugs. "I hope you like it. I tend to make it stronger than what it says in the instructions."

Nate lifted his mug and took a tentative sip. The flavor combination was perfect. "It's great. Thank you."

She nodded and took a sip of her own, her gaze resting on Seth and Jordan. "Where did Minnie go?"

"I think we wore her out. She's asleep in the living room." Nate pointed toward the table where the boys were enjoying their treats. Jordan's eyelids were growing heavy, however, and even Seth wasn't nearly as energetic as he usually was. "I'm betting they both sleep well tonight."

"I sure hope so." She lifted her mug to her lips and glanced at him over the top, the steam partially obscuring her eyes. They were red, and the area beneath them was a little puffy. He was right. She had been crying.

Guilt took another stab at his gut. He needed to talk to her about it. To apologize and repair things as best he could. The thought of their friendship suffering was something he couldn't accept.

As if she could read his mind, Bailey took a sip of her hot chocolate and eyed him warily. "I should probably get dinner started."

"We need to talk, Bailey."

"I can't. Not now." She curled both hands around her mug as though she were desperately trying to absorb the warmth.

He wished he knew if she meant because the boys were within hearing distance or if she didn't want to talk at all. Instead of pressuring her, he let the subject drop and prayed that God would somehow help make everything right.

Bailey pulled a baking sheet out from the drawer under the stove and got the butter out of the fridge. She placed slices of bread on the baking sheet and began to butter them.

Nate stood and set his mug on the counter. "What can I do?"

She got a soup pot out of the cabinet and handed it to him. "There are a couple of cans of chicken noodle soup in the pantry. Right in front on the middle shelf."

They worked on dinner as Seth and Jordan finished their hot chocolate.

After dinner, Bailey set up a board game, and the four of them played one round of Chutes and Ladders before it was time for the boys to take baths and go to bed.

Seth gave Nate a hug. "I'm real glad you and Minnie are here. I wish you could live here all the time." With a big grin, he turned and dashed up the stairs.

Jordan gave him a wordless hug and followed his brother.

Before joining her sons, Bailey turned toward Nate. "I need some time to process. I'm confused, and I feel like a horrible person." Her voice caught.

Boy, he could relate. "If it helps, I feel the same way."

With a little nod, she went upstairs, leaving Nate in the dining room that suddenly seemed way too cold and quiet.

He gathered the mugs and took them to the sink, where several other dishes were waiting. The least he could do was clean up the kitchen while she was gone. After that, he'd have to find a way to focus on something else. As if it were possible to stop thinking about their kiss or the mess it may have created.

His cell phone rang, the name on the caller ID surprising him. "Bailey?"

"I just looked out my bedroom window to see if it was still raining, and I think I saw someone lurking by the tree swing and watching the house."

Chapter Twenty-Two

As soon as Bailey spotted the glowing red light along the tree line, she tried to casually close the blinds in her bedroom window, and then she quickly called Nate. If someone was watching the house—watching her—she didn't want to tip them off to the fact that she'd noticed them.

A tap on her door made her jump. She strode across the room and opened it, allowing Nate inside. Minnie trotted through the doorway after him.

Nate scanned her from head to toe. "You okay?"

"Yeah. But if someone's out there watching the house, how long have they been there? And what are they waiting for?" She shivered, thankful she hadn't yet changed out of her warm clothes from earlier.

"Turn off the lights. That way, they won't be able to see us. Then come to the window and try to show me what you saw."

Nate waited for her by the window, then slowly lifted the blinds away from the wall on one side.

Bailey stepped up beside him and pointed. "It was

down there, by the tire swing. A red light that seemed to glow and fade."

She remembered the day Joe hung up that swing. The boys played on it regularly. The thought that someone might be lurking nearby made her feel sick.

They stood in silence for a while, but the red light never did reappear. She sagged against the wall and used a thumb to rub circles against her temple. "I promise I saw something, Nate."

He let the blinds rest against the window and turned to face her. "I believe you. Most likely, whoever it was saw you looking out the window and was afraid they'd been spotted. Probably long gone by now. I'll take Minnie and check it out."

Her eyes widened. "But what if they didn't leave? What if they're still out there and see you coming?"

He led the way downstairs to the kitchen and paused at the back door. "We've got more rain in the forecast. If we wait until morning, we might lose any evidence that could be out there." He pulled his phone out and then withdrew an AirPod from his pocket. "I want you to lock this door behind me and then go back upstairs. I'm going to call you and stay on the line. Let me know if you see any movement."

"That's a good idea." When he called her number, she answered and pressed the phone to her ear with a nod. Now that he had it connected to his AirPod, he slid his phone back into his pocket, leaving both hands free. He held Minnie's leash in one along with a small flashlight and gripped his gun in the other.

For the second time since he'd come to the house, she shut and locked the door behind him. "I'm going back upstairs now."

"Good. Let me know when you're at the window."

She took the stairs two at a time and re-entered her room, careful to keep the light off so she could see outside. "I'm here."

"Tell me if you see any movement at all."

"I will. Please be careful." The thought of him getting hurt made her feel sick.

"Always."

She could easily see Nate and Minnie as they crossed the yard, his flashlight illuminating their way. She uttered a silent prayer for their safety and that, if there was any evidence out there, Nate would find it.

His voice, just above a whisper, sounded in her ear. "See anything?"

"No. Nothing."

"Okay, I want you to guide me to where you saw the light. With all this rain, it's possible someone might have left footprints behind."

He'd believed her without question, and that fact warmed her heart.

"It looked like it was close to that big oak where the tire swing is. Either beside it or just back a ways. It was hard to tell."

"That's great. I'm almost there."

Bailey watched as his light bobbed in the distance, pausing when he reached the tree line. She held her breath and squinted into the darkness.

"Minnie can smell something interesting, but she's not barking. Whoever was here probably got spooked and left."

A mixture of relief and disappointment collided as Bailey released the breath she'd been holding.

"We've got some footprints. Rain is going to wash these

away. I'm going to try to get a few pictures before that happens. Hang on."

Several moments passed while he took photos, and Bailey could see the flash from her vantage point. She was glad he'd found something, but now she just wanted him to return to the house where he was safe. Meanwhile, her eyes kept scanning the tree line and praying that the person who'd been there wasn't doubling back.

"Okay, we're heading your way."

"Thank goodness." She watched from the window until he was two-thirds of the way back. Then she hurried downstairs and opened the door for him.

Minnie trotted inside, shook, and then sat patiently until Nate re-holstered his gun and removed her leash.

He held up one hand triumphantly, a blue glove in his palm. "I found the source of the red light. There were four cigarette butts on the ground near the footprints. One was still smoldering. He was there for a while."

"He? You're sure?" She eyed the glove. "Do you always have gloves with you?"

He shrugged. "A habit I picked up from our medical examiner at the precinct a couple of years back. It's come in handy. And yes, I'm sure. I'll show you why, but first, do you have a plastic bag I can put these cigarette butts in?"

She retrieved one from the drawer near the refrigerator and held it open so he could drop them in. Once she'd sealed the bag, she placed it on the counter.

Nate pulled his phone out and went to his pictures. "Unless a woman was wearing oversized boots, this guy's feet are larger than mine."

There were a couple of close-up photos of the footprints showing the tread. Another photo showed Nate's shoe next to the imprint. Whoever was out there had feet at least a size bigger.

Bailey shuddered, remembering the way the red glow had pulsed in and out before fading completely. He must have seen her in the window, known there was a possibility she would spot the cigarette burning and left.

"The good news is, the lab can run DNA on the cigarettes. At the very least, we'll get confirmation on whether it was a man. If his DNA is in the system, we may even get an ID." Nate smiled triumphantly. "This could be the break we needed. I'll go back out once the sun's up to get a better look. Then I'll take the evidence in to the department first thing."

She breathed a sigh of relief. "That's great." She wrapped her arms around herself, suddenly chilled. "I wish I knew why he was watching us. It's downright creepy."

"Yeah, it's pretty messed up." He started to reach out a hand but stopped himself and stuffed both into the pockets of his jeans. "Look, I'd rather stay here myself and make sure you and the boys are okay, but after what happened earlier, I wanted you to know I understand if you need Jenny to take my place."

Bailey immediately shook her head. "That isn't necessary. The boys feel safe with you here, and so do I."

"I'm glad." He seemed to be weighing his next words. "I'm sorry I upset you. Hurting you is the last thing in the world I want to do. You and your friendship mean the world to me. I wouldn't intentionally jeopardize that for anything." His gaze pinned her in place, his brown eyes pleading with her to understand.

"It was just as much my fault." Her words were barely above a whisper. Even as she spoke, the memory of being wrapped in his arms was impossible to shake. She felt safer

—more cared for—in those moments than she had since Joe... She felt horrible for even thinking about it. "I don't want our friendship to change either."

She wanted to go upstairs and escape the uncomfortableness between them, but if they were truly going to pretend the kiss hadn't happened, she needed to make the first move. "I don't think I'll be able to go to sleep for a while. Why don't I get my laptop so I can do some research while we watch TV?"

"That sounds like a great idea."

Upstairs in her room, she crossed the space to look out the window again. There was no sign of the man who'd been watching them before, but a shiver still traveled up her spine. What was he waiting for?

Chapter Twenty-Three

From the look of exhaustion on Bailey's face, Nate doubted she slept much at all last night. Was it because of the intruder outside? Or was it related to their conversation? Goodness knew both had kept him up much of the night as well.

What he'd said about not wanting to jeopardize their friendship was true. What he didn't voice was that it'd been difficult to ignore his feelings before. Now that he knew what it felt like to hold and kiss her, pretending that it hadn't happened was going to be torture.

He was relieved, however, when she'd come downstairs with a smile on her face as she'd greeted him this morning.

Now, she was making scrambled eggs and hash browns while Seth and Jordan waited patiently at the table for their breakfast.

"I heard from Rachel this morning," she told Nate as she stirred the eggs. "She's going to stop by later today to help out for a while."

"That's great." He pulled two slices of bread from the

toaster and buttered them. "I can run the evidence over to the police department while she's here." He'd feel better knowing someone else was at the store with Bailey and the boys.

He got a stack of plates out of the cabinet while Bailey retrieved forks.

This was only their second morning in the same house, and he couldn't ignore how well they worked together. He was going to miss spending so much time with her and the boys once everything got back to normal. It was going to be difficult going back to only seeing them a couple of times a month.

They ate breakfast in comfortable conversation, mostly revolving around looking for frogs after last night's rain and cleaning up the store.

When they'd finished, Nate left Bailey to wash dishes and headed back out to the spot where the man had been watching last night. Now that it was daylight, maybe he'd be able to see more evidence. He took two baggies with him just in case.

The rain had washed away the footprints just as he'd feared it would. He was glad he'd taken photographs. There were still a few cigarette butts on the ground where he'd found the others. He took some more pictures and left them there just in case someone from the station wanted to see the location.

After that, he walked along the tree line all around the house and found two more places with discarded cigarette butts. Whoever that man was, he'd been watching the house for a while and from multiple vantage points. Anger burned, and concern flared. He was even more thankful she'd agreed to let him stay at the house.

He took photographs of each location as well as a photo

of the house so that he'd have a record of what angles the guy was watching.

Back at the house, Bailey, Seth, and Jordan were getting ready to head out to check on animals and then go work on the store. While her sons were busy deciding which toys to take with them, Nate pulled her aside and told her what he'd found.

"I'd like to come with you guys to check on the animals. After that, please do me a favor and make sure you lock the doors while you're working at the store. Until we catch this guy, don't let the boys out to play by themselves. I'd rather be safe."

Bailey nodded, her expression serious. "I agree on all counts. I'm not even sure we should be walking anywhere at this point."

He'd been thinking along the same lines. He doubted the suspect had been watching them on the way to the old barn last night because Minnie would've noticed. Still, just the idea was disconcerting.

"If you're okay with it, I'll leave Minnie here at the house while we're all gone. Trust me, no one will mess with it while she's here."

●

Nate was able to leave the farm early because Rachel was already waiting at the store when they arrived. Even knowing Bailey wasn't there alone, he still hoped to get back as soon as possible.

Walking in the front door of the Destiny Police Department was somewhat surreal. He hadn't been there since he'd taken his leave last February. To be honest, he'd avoided it. Part of him had worried that returning would stir up some of the anger and grief he'd experienced after Lana's death. What he hadn't expected was the strong sense of home that it elicited.

Tia was manning one of the windows and was helping someone who'd come in. She looked up and spotted him, giving him an enthusiastic wave. He grinned in response and pointed to the door that, when buzzed open, would lead to the bullpen beyond.

Tia nodded. A moment later, the lock clicked, and Nate pushed his way through. There were a lot of new faces, but plenty of officers he'd worked with before greeted him and shook his hand. It took ten minutes to make his way through to Detective Paris's office. He knocked on the doorframe.

Paris stood and waved him in. "Hey, Walker. Good to see you. Glad you came in—it's been too long."

"Yeah, it has." Nate shook the detective's hand and took a seat across the desk from him. "We had some interesting developments last night, and I thought I'd come by and give a report personally. I've got some evidence to log in as well."

Paris raised an eyebrow. "I can't wait to hear about it." He looked up as a shadow darkened the doorway.

Nate turned to find Chief Arnold Dolman standing there. Nate got to his feet and shook the chief's hand. "Good to see you, sir."

"You too, Nate. It's a real shame what Bailey is going through. I'm glad that she's got you in her corner." Chief Dolman jabbed a thumb behind him. "Mind stopping by my office on your way out?"

"Not at all, sir. I'll be right there."

"Great. See you in a bit." With that, Chief Dolman left again.

Paris fought a smile. "Back for a half hour and already in trouble with the chief. Old habits die hard."

"Funny, Paris." Nate acted offended, but really, he enjoyed the teasing. He'd missed these guys and hadn't realized just how much.

He placed the bags of cigarette butts on Paris's desk and went on to give an account of what happened from the moment Bailey spotted the red glow until Nate had a chance to investigate the area in the daylight.

"I was hoping we might get some DNA off these cigarette butts. Most may have been out during the rainstorm. But this one should be good." He pointed out the one he'd found smoldering last night. "I'd definitely have the lab test that one first."

Paris nodded and seemed impressed. "I'll be sure they get there myself. With any luck, the DNA profile will match someone in our database, and we'll have a name in the next few hours."

"I sure hope so. Bailey's been through a lot over the last couple of years. She shouldn't have to deal with this on top of it all."

"No, she shouldn't." Paris's voice was firm with conviction. "Is there anything we can do to help her?"

"Actually, I do have an idea, and I wanted to run it by you first."

He explained his plans and was happy when Paris agreed with him and promised to help set everything in motion.

Nate stood. He wanted to get back to the farm, but he still needed to stop in and see the chief on his way out. "There's one last thing. Has anyone done a check on the property and the last few people who owned it? Specifically, I'd really like to know more about the large barn that's barely still standing and what happened to the owners who built it."

"I'll get someone on that today." Paris held out a hand. "Keep me updated, and I'll do the same. Stop by anytime. We've missed you around here."

"Thanks, I'll have to do that." The men shook hands, and Nate headed out.

He was waylaid by two other people who wanted to say hello before he made it to the chief's office. "You wanted to see me, sir?"

"Come on in and close the door."

Nate did as he was asked and took a seat. He wasn't sure what the chief wanted to talk about, so he started off with small talk. "How are Chloe and the baby doing?"

Chief Dolman's face lit up. "They're great. Thank you." He picked up a framed photo and handed it to Nate. The baby girl was adorable with hair the same dark blonde as her mom's. "Etta is five weeks old now and changing every day. Chloe and I are sleep-deprived but elated." He chuckled.

"That's great to hear, sir."

"I'm thankful that you, Durant, and Paris are doing so much to help Bailey. She's still one of ours, and it upsets me that someone is messing with her like this."

"Me, too, sir. We're doing everything we can to catch whoever's behind all of this."

"I know you are, which brings me to why I asked you in here. I hear you're doing great things through Paws with a Cause. They're lucky to have you." Chief Dolman paused as he studied Nate. "Now that you're essentially working a case, have you given any thought to returning to the PD?"

The chief never was one to beat around the bush for long. Then again, that's partly why it made him so good at his job.

"I'm not going to lie. I've missed working with everyone, and I'm feeling the loss even more now that I've been back in the building." Nate tried to choose his words carefully. "But I'm not sure I'm ready to come back. Not yet."

"I hope that means you might consider it in the future. If that *is* the case, please know you'll always have a place back here if you want it."

"I appreciate that. Truly. Thank you, sir."

"You're welcome." Chief Dolman stood and extended a hand. "I'll let you get back to it. Keep the department updated."

Nate shook the chief's hand. "Will do. Please tell Chloe I said hello. Congratulations to you both again."

By the time he got back out to his truck, he was ready to check on Bailey and the boys. He'd kept his phone handy but never got a call or text from her. Hopefully, that meant she and Rachel were busy working on the store and that everything was going smoothly.

He prayed that they'd hear from the station in the next few hours with some good news after the evidence was processed.

Chapter Twenty-Four

For the fifth time in an hour, Jordan flopped into Bailey's lap, where she was sitting on the floor, and leaned his head back against her chest. The poor kid was bored, and she couldn't blame him. At the same time, she needed to get as much done as possible before lunch.

She wrapped her arms around him and gave him a cuddle. "Why don't you go choose a toy or puzzle out of the toy bin? Since we don't have any customers today, you can even drive your Hot Wheels cars around the front of the store." She pointed to the plastic bin on the floor near the little table.

Jordan had brought a book and an action figure with him today, but he'd gotten bored with them quickly. He shook his head and didn't move from her lap. She looked at the stack of greeting cards and envelopes beside her.

The guy who'd broken into the place had knocked the entire display over. Thankfully, with the exception of a few dirty envelopes, most of them could be saved. Now, she had to separate them by style and get them back on the display.

"You've been working hard for hours anyway," Rachel said from her spot on the other side of the room. She'd been sweeping up broken glass from several shattered mugs. "It'd do you good to take a break."

Jordan leaned his head back and looked at her as if to say, "Yeah, Mom."

"Maybe when Nate gets back, we can go out somewhere for lunch. Just to do something different."

Her suggestion was met with cheers from both boys.

"Can we get cheeseburgers?" The question came from Seth.

"We'll see."

With that news, Jordan scrambled from Bailey's lap and went to see what his brother was doing.

"You're welcome to join us, Rachel, if you'd like."

"I appreciate the invitation, but I'll probably go home for lunch. I'm happy to come back afterward if you need me." Rachel glanced around the store. "There's still a lot to do."

"Yeah, there is. But I've come to the realization that we're not going to be ready to open by Friday. In which case, there's no hurry. So feel free to call it done when you're ready to leave for lunch."

"All right, but only if you're sure." The older woman shook her head. "I'll never understand why someone would go to all this effort. I mean, seriously. Didn't they have anything better to do?"

"Apparently not." Bailey grimaced. "I guess it gives me an excuse to look for some new inventory, though. I'll have to get to that once I've found someone to level that old barn."

Rachel looked up in surprise. "You're finally going to demolish it?"

"I figured it was about time. It would be the perfect spot for a huge pumpkin patch next fall. Don't you think?"

"I think it'd be great. People love that kind of thing in the fall." Rachel ran a hand through her short, gray hair. "You might be able to find someone willing to keep materials and knock it down at a cheaper rate. Surely, there's something in there worth salvaging. It'd be worth asking about, anyway."

"I'll have to do that. Thanks for the suggestion."

Bailey no sooner heard an engine out front than Seth ran to the door.

"Nate's back!"

"Nate!" Jordan ran from his spot and practically jumped at Nate the moment the poor guy walked in.

He easily swooped the boy into his arms, chuckling. "Wow, that's quite a welcome. I didn't know you guys missed me so much."

"We're going to go get cheeseburgers now that you're back," Seth declared proudly.

"I see how it is. That's okay. Cheeseburgers are pretty high on my priority list, too." He tickled Jordan and set him down before looking at Bailey.

When he smiled at her, Bailey's stomach did a little flip. She chided herself as she smiled back. "The boys were getting restless. I thought going out for lunch might help."

"That sounds great. Count me in." He turned his attention to Seth. "What are you working on, buddy? Need help finishing it before we go eat?" The duo moved away with Jordan trailing them.

Rachel drifted closer to Bailey and lowered her voice. "What's going on with the two of you?"

Bailey's eyes widened. "What are you talking about?"

The older woman grinned. "There's something

different about the way you're interacting with each other. For the record, I think it's a good idea."

With her cheeks on fire, Bailey put a stack of cards on the display and tried to ignore the sensation. "Well, I'm not so sure."

She glanced at Nate, who was helping Seth sweep up some debris.

"You just need to have an open mind. I'm pretty sure he's already crazy about you." Rachel reached out and gave Bailey's arm a squeeze. "You guys enjoy lunch, and I'll touch base with you all tomorrow."

"Sounds good. Thanks again, Rachel."

With a wave and some quick hugs for the boys, Rachel retrieved her purse and left.

Bailey replaced the rest of the greeting cards and nodded in satisfaction. It was one step closer to being able to open to the public again.

"It looks good." Nate's voice came from near her right elbow.

"Thanks. Slowly but surely getting there, right?"

"Progress is progress, and you're getting things knocked out one by one."

Bailey nodded her agreement. "How'd it go at the station? Was it weird being back?"

"A little. I thought it would bother me more than it did." His voice trailed off. "Detective Paris encouraged me to come back, and the chief said my job was waiting if I ever made that decision."

"That's pretty cool. Nice to know, regardless of what the future holds."

"Yeah, it is." He shifted his weight. "I handed over the evidence. Paris said they'll run the DNA through the system. If there's a match, we should know in a few hours. He promised to call when they have something."

"So now we wait."

He gave her elbow a gentle nudge with his own. "I need to run over and let Minnie outside for a few minutes. Then will you be ready to eat?"

"Absolutely. I'm starving."

●

Nate's suggestion to eat at The Corner Café proved to be an excellent one. Bailey and Jordan were sitting on the bench on one side of the table, while Nate and Seth were sitting in chairs on the other.

Seth and Jordan split a large cheeseburger and scarfed it down in no time. Now they were across from each other and using french fries and ketchup to paint a roadway on the paper place mat between them. She ought to scold them about the mess, but they weren't getting ketchup on the table, and it was keeping them entertained. Plus, they were playing together, which was always nice to see.

Seth looked up from his handiwork. "Can we take Minnie some french fries? I bet she's sad that she couldn't come here with us."

With a grin, Nate tipped his basket to show a small pile of fries that'd been left on one side. "Way ahead of you. Good dogs should always get some french fries."

That made Seth happy, and he went back to his ketchup art.

Nate's phone pinged, and he glanced at the screen. His brow furrowed.

"What is it?"

"Just heard back from Paris. They already got the DNA results back."

"That was fast. Is it unusual to get results so quickly?"

"Not if Paris put a rush on it." He glanced at Seth and then moved around the table to sit on the bench next to Bailey. He held the phone out so she could read the text.

"*DNA results are in. Our suspect is a man, but there were no matches in the system.*"

Bailey tried to squelch her disappointment, but it wasn't working. "So we're back to square one again."

Nate leaned closer, his arm pressing against hers. "The good news is, now his DNA *is* in the system. If he messes up in the future, it'll get matched to your case, and Paris will be alerted. It's another step in the right direction. He messed up when he let you see him and again when he left evidence behind. It won't be long before he makes an even bigger mistake. We're going to catch him."

She nodded, drawing reassurance and strength from him. She couldn't help wondering, though, why their suspect wasn't in the system. Maybe it was a good sign, and the guy wasn't a hardened criminal.

Or was it only because he hadn't been caught yet?

Chapter Twenty-Five

The whole ride home from lunch, Bailey had been unusually quiet. Nate tried to start a conversation several times, but her answers were brief and scattered. He finally turned the music up, letting the boys sing along to one of their favorite songs and giving her the peace she seemed to need.

He pulled into the drive leading to the front gate and stopped to punch in the code. That's when he noticed a large cardboard box sitting on the ground beside the mailbox.

"Bailey? Are you expecting any packages?"

"What?" His question seemed to break her out of her reverie. She leaned forward to look. "I don't know. Maybe. We have several companies that send us new products to stock in the store on commission. It could be from one of them." She released her seat belt and opened the passenger door before Nate could offer to get it for her.

She retrieved the mail from the mailbox and set it in the console. Then she went back for the box. It was the size of two shoeboxes lying side by side. "Weird. There's no label on this." She lifted it toward the cab of the truck.

"Bailey, wait—"

She screamed and dropped the box again, practically jumping into the truck, her breath coming in gasps.

"Mom? What's wrong?" Seth leaned forward in his booster seat.

Bailey looked at Nate, her eyes wide. "Something moved in the box after I picked it up. I think there's something alive in there." She gave a violent shudder.

Nate threw the truck into park. "You guys stay in here."

He jogged around the vehicle. The box had landed on the ground, one corner propped up by a large rock. Nate nudged it with the toe of his shoe and immediately heard something shift around inside.

He dialed Paris's number. The detective answered on the second ring.

"Paris here."

"Hey, it's Nate. We've got a suspicious package out in front of Bailey's place—no label or return address. There may be a living creature inside. Something's definitely moving around in there."

"Steer clear of it. I'm sending a unit your way."

With that, the connection ended. He got back into the truck. "The police are on their way. While we wait, let's take a look at the camera footage and see if we can figure out who left it."

"What if there's a puppy in the box?" The question came from Seth. "Or a guinea pig?"

"Or a rhino." Jordan cackled at his suggestion. "A biiiiig rhino."

Nate looked in the mirror at the youngster. "That would be quite the magic trick, wouldn't it?" He glanced over to see Bailey smiling at her son's antics in spite of her worry.

He half listened as the boys went through idea after idea, trying to one-up each other.

"Here we go." Nate positioned the phone between them. Bailey leaned in so she could see the screen, too. She rested an elbow on the console, the sleeve of her shirt tickling his arm. "Here's the first recorded footage."

They watched as a woman in a postal service uniform placed several envelopes and flyers in the mailbox and closed it again. She walked away immediately and didn't return with the box.

"That's our normal mail lady," Bailey confirmed. "She's been delivering in this area for over a year now."

"Let's see what this second recording is. It looks like maybe ten minutes after the mail was delivered." He started the next video. Both he and Bailey leaned in closer, their heads nearly touching.

A man walked into the frame, a large-brimmed hat pulled low over his ears and blocking any view of his face. Thanks to a long-sleeved shirt and dark pants, there was no way to see any distinguishable marks.

He carefully set the box on the ground and backed out of the frame.

"He had gloves on," Bailey said, a hint of defeat in her voice. "There aren't going to be fingerprints."

Nate backed the video up and hit play again. "True. But look." He paused it and pointed to the man's feet. "Boots. Maybe there's a footprint out there that we can compare to the ones we found in the woods near your house. It won't be conclusive, but it should give us a good idea if this is the same man."

"You're right. And just because he wore gloves when he

brought the box doesn't mean he did when filling and sealing it." She sat back in her seat again as he scrolled through the other camera feeds. "What are you doing?"

"Making sure no one's messed with the store or house. At least not blatantly. As soon as the police arrive, I'll drive you and the kids home, make sure you're set, and then come back. It could take a while. There's no use you guys waiting around here." Truthfully, he didn't want them anywhere near here when they finally opened the box.

Bailey's eyes narrowed as she studied him. Apparently, she'd picked up on something in his tone. "What are they going to do with the box?"

"They need to cover their bases. Use a metal detector to make sure there's nothing dangerous inside."

"Like a b-o-m-b." She spelled the word so that the boys wouldn't overhear. "Is that a possibility?"

"Highly unlikely. But it's protocol when dealing with a strange and unknown package. Just a precaution."

She nodded but didn't look convinced.

Nate was relieved when a police car pulled up behind them, shortly followed by another. Jenny got out and came to the driver's window.

"You guys okay?"

"I'm going to take them to the house and come back. The package is over there by the mailbox. We did get a video of the man dropping it off. No visual of his face, though. I'll make sure to get that video to you and Paris."

"Sounds good." Jenny looked past Nate to Bailey. "Try not to worry. We'll come by as soon as we're done here."

When they got to the house, Minnie greeted them enthusiastically at the door. That meant the house was secure, and Nate had no problem dropping Bailey and the kids off.

The boys ran upstairs to their bedrooms.

"I'll keep you in the loop," Nate promised. "I'll be back as soon as possible." He turned to leave and was nearly out the door when Bailey's urgent tone stopped him.

"Nate?"

He faced her again to find her watching him, her arms wrapped around her torso.

"I need..." Her voice faltered. "Please be careful."

Nate didn't allow himself to second-guess his instincts. He strode forward and wrapped her in his arms. The moment she leaned into him and gripped his waist, he knew he'd done the right thing. "I promise. Everything's going to be fine." He pressed a light kiss to her temple.

She nodded against his chest.

Nate took a step back, gave her shoulder a gentle squeeze, and headed back to the front gate.

By the time he got there, Officer Philip Lorenzo was carefully going over the package with a metal detector. If there was a scene with a possible bomb, he was the one who was called in. It was only moments before he shook his head and stepped back. "You're clear."

Detective Paris must have arrived while Nate was taking Bailey and the boys to the house. He gave Jenny her cue. With a pair of latex gloves on, she took out a knife and carefully cut along the edges of the box lid to loosen the cardboard. When she was done, she sheathed the knife and began to lift one flap of the box.

A persistent rattle—almost like a hiss—caused her to jump backward, putting plenty of space between her and the box.

"Detective, I think we're going to need animal control out here. I'm pretty sure there's a rattlesnake in the box."

Chapter Twenty-Six

There had been two young rattlesnakes in the box. No matter how many times Bailey repeated the fact to herself, she could hardly believe it. If she'd taken the box in and opened it without taking precautions, she could've been bitten. Or the snakes might have gotten loose and bitten one of the boys.

To top it all off, there was no note included with the snakes. Not even a threat, although the fact that someone had gone to the effort to capture venomous snakes and deliver them to her house was threat enough.

She'd even gone through the mail from the mailbox in case a note had been placed there separately. Still nothing.

They'd found some footprints around the mailbox, and Nate had taken pictures of each one. Now, all the officers had gone home except for Jenny. She and Nate were sitting on the couch, Nate's laptop open on the coffee table in front of them.

"What about this one?" Jenny pointed to the screen.

Bailey rounded the couch to stand behind them where she could see.

Nate glanced up at her. "I've got the footprint from the guy last night here," he pointed to the image on the left, "and we're comparing it to pictures I took by the mailbox. I'm hoping we'll find a match." He closed that picture and opened another. The tread was clearly different. He opened yet another and stopped. "Just like that."

Bailey leaned forward, her forearms resting on the back of the couch between Nate and Jenny. There was no doubt that they were both created from the same shoe or boot. "Definitely a match. So it was the same guy."

Jenny gave a shake of her head. "Judging from the fact that we never saw his face on video, he didn't care if the camera caught him. This means he's confident that we can't identify him by his clothing or hat alone. He's bold yet careful."

"Not the best combination," Nate muttered. "Eventually, he's going to get overconfident and make a mistake. We're going to be there when that happens."

Bailey pushed away from the couch. "Well, everything before was bad enough, but the rattlesnakes crossed a line. Someone could've been seriously injured. What is he going to try next?"

It made her angry to think this guy was trying to make her upset enough to sell her place. Yet, there was a small part of her that wondered if it was worth it to keep fighting. She was tired, and the farm was a lot. But if she did let it go, how would she support the boys? She'd have to get a job and start working, and the only thing on her resume since Seth was born was stay-at-home mom and running the farm. There wasn't a big call for either when it came to employment.

Suddenly, the stress of it all made her want to curl up on her bed, have a good cry, and drown it all in a big tub of ice cream. She cleared her throat. "I'm going to check on the boys. I'll be back in a few minutes."

"Bailey? Are you okay?"

Nate's concerned voice only brought the tears closer to the surface. Not trusting her voice, she gave a wave and made her way upstairs. In the hallway, she took several deep breaths and blinked back the tears before peeking her head into Seth's room.

The boys were sitting at the little table with a bunch of building blocks and toy farm animals.

Seth's sweet face brightened when he saw her. "Mom, look what we're building." He stood and swept his hand over the table as though he were beginning a presentation. "We're building the old barn in the woods. Except we fixed everything, and now there's lots of room for more animals. See? Even Poppy, Petunia, and Pansy have their own bedrooms."

Bailey couldn't help but smile at the vision of each goat having a fancy four-post bed to sleep on. "I love it. Very creative, you two. Are you going to give the barn a name?"

Seth touched his chin with his index finger and thought for a moment. "The Hidden Barn. Don't you think that's a good name?"

"It's great, honey. It's nice to see you guys playing together so well."

Seth lowered his voice. "I'm mostly letting Jordan add the roof pieces. The other stuff is a little too hard for him."

She chuckled. "Well, you're both doing a great job. I'm going to let you guys get back to your building and go downstairs. Love you."

She'd barely made it to the door before Seth spoke again.

"Hey, Mom?"

"Yeah, baby?"

"I like having Nate around. I wish he didn't have to go back to his house."

Jordan looked up for the first time and nodded. "Me, too."

Bailey was getting used to him being there, too. Before this, they saw him once a week at the most. Sometimes, it went as long as a month between visits. What if it went back to that once this mess was over and he returned to his normal routine again? One way or another—whether they caught this guy or not—Nate would be back to work on Monday. "I know what you guys mean. But the important thing is that we all live in the same town. Maybe he can come over for pizza sometimes."

"Or cheeseburgers," Seth said in agreement.

"All right, you guys keep on having fun."

With that, she left them to their building and crossed the hallway to her own bedroom.

Standing in front of the large mirror against one wall, she looked at her reflection and frowned.

The boys kept her plenty busy during the day. The truth was, though, the evenings and nights were terrible. They were way too quiet, lonely, and sometimes downright creepy. Having this huge house felt like too much when all the creaks and groans made her feel jumpy. And that was before someone was trying to scare her out of her home.

Would she ever be able to relax again after this case was solved?

A dog of their own very well might be a must. But a house all on one level would be really nice, too. If they stayed here, she would look into having a security system installed.

There were a lot of ifs there. Was she actually seriously considering selling the place?

Her gaze flicked to the framed photo on her dresser. She and Joe were smiling for the camera. What the picture didn't show was how Joe had his hand poised just inches from her ribs and that, as soon as the photo was taken, he'd tickled her.

The memory made her smile, but it quickly morphed back into a frown.

"Would you hate me if I sold this place?" As soon as the words were uttered, she knew the answer was no. He would want her to be happy. Safe. He would have supported her in anything she truly wanted to do.

Was she willing to walk away from the place that held so many memories that she shared with Joe? That was the real question. Why couldn't it all be black and white?

She took a deep breath and headed back downstairs. When she re-entered the living room, both Nate and Jenny looked up from their conversation, concern evident on their faces.

"I was just going to come up and check on you." Jenny stood. "I know today's been a lot. Maybe I should head home and give you a chance to relax a little this afternoon and evening."

Bailey swallowed hard. "Joe had so many plans for our future here. Would I be dishonoring his memory if I sold this place? Would I be severing one of the last connections between him and the boys?" Her voice cracked, and her face flushed. She never should've voiced her concerns. Her friends were going to think she was finally losing it. Maybe she was.

Chapter Twenty-Seven

Jenny strode across the living room and gave Bailey a tight hug. "Are you serious? Of course you wouldn't be dishonoring his memory. My goodness, Bailey. All he wanted was for you and the boys to be happy."

Another hand touched her back and she let Nate's warmth and calming presence wash over her.

"Joe once told me that he liked the idea of the farm because he hoped the two of you would eventually be able to work together. I don't think he would've cared if it'd been here or if you'd bought and run a pizzeria." His voice was gruff. "It was always about spending time with you and the boys."

Jenny leaned back and looked Bailey in the eyes. "As far as keeping Joe's memory alive for Seth and Jordan? You, my friend, are that connection. Not this house or that lamp on the table or even the tire swing outside. You. The stories you'll tell them, pictures you'll show them. You're the one who's going to keep Joe alive for them. And do you know what?" She paused dramatically. "You can do that from anywhere."

Bailey chuckled and swiped at her tears. Heat suffused her cheeks as she cast a glance at Nate. "I'm sorry. I promise I don't normally cry this much." She pressed her hands against her face and willed herself to stop blushing.

"Are you kidding? You're a beautiful person inside and out, no matter what." The words left his lips, and he seemed surprised that he'd spoken them out loud.

Jenny nodded. "I couldn't agree more." She glanced from Nate to Bailey. "You've got to give yourself a little grace, girl. You've earned it." She gave Nate a pointed look.

He dropped his hand from the small of Bailey's back. "Why don't I check on the boys for a few minutes? Make sure they're not getting into too much trouble." He let out a whistle and led the way upstairs, Minnie on his heels.

As soon as he was gone, Jenny placed her hands on Bailey's shoulders. "This isn't just about the farm, is it?"

"What do you mean?" Bailey stepped away to retrieve a tissue from a box on a nearby table. She blew her nose and then grabbed another to swipe at her eyes.

When she turned back, Jenny was standing there, hands on her hips, with an unconvinced look on her face. "I've known you and Nate long enough to see something's shifted. You two are acting differently toward each other. Did something happen?"

Bailey shrugged, but her face must have revealed the truth.

Jenny slapped a hand over her mouth to cover a surprised gasp. "Something *did* happen. I knew it."

Bailey glanced at the stairs and lowered her voice. "We kissed yesterday."

Her friend looked excited and then sobered. "Are you okay?"

"Honestly? I don't know. Like you, Nate's one of my best friends. The idea of something ruining that makes me physically sick."

"The fact that you're such good friends is a big plus. Nate knows exactly what you've been going through. He's been there for you and the boys. I mean, as soon as he knew you were in danger, he was ready to do anything in order to keep you guys safe."

"I know." Bailey groaned. "Then there's Joe. We're talking about his best friend here. I should feel horribly guilty for even thinking about this, much less for how I'm starting to feel toward Nate. But I don't. Which makes me feel even worse." She gave a half sob, half laugh. "I'm an absolute mess. Seriously."

"You need to talk to Nate. I guarantee you, he's having similar struggles, wondering if Joe would think he's stealing his girl. Hoping that you don't think less of him for caring about you that way."

Bailey blinked at her friend. "Has he said anything about it to you?"

"No. He's never said a word, but I know him just like I know you." Jenny led the way back to the couch where they both took a seat. "Talk to Nate. Pray about it. Most importantly, leave your heart open to the possibilities. Not just with Nate but with where you want to live and what you want to do. Don't let guilt rob you of the future God wants you to have."

Bailey nodded, her friend's advice beginning to sink in. "I'll think about it. Thank you." She reached over and gave Jenny a hug. "You're a straight shooter. Have I ever told you how much I appreciate that?"

"I'm glad because my mom says that's why I haven't landed a man yet." Jenny laughed, but it was obvious she meant what she said.

"Your mom is a sweet lady, but sometimes I wonder about her."

"You and me both." Jenny gave her another quick hug. "Seriously, I'm going to get out of your hair for a while. Give you a chance to talk to Nate or put your feet up for a while. But you know I'm only a phone call away, right?"

"Yeah. I know. Thanks, my friend."

"You're welcome." She cupped her hands around her mouth and hollered toward the stairs. "I'm heading out, guys. Maybe I'll see you tomorrow."

Moments later, it sounded like a herd of elephants were stomping down the stairs. The boys appeared at the bottom, followed by Nate. They all gave Jenny a hug before she left with a smile and a wave.

Bailey closed the door behind her and took in a cleansing breath as Seth and Jordan bounded toward her.

"We're hungry," Seth announced. "And bored. Can we play a game?"

"Or watch TV?" Jordan looked up at her hopefully. "Please?"

Bailey was bone weary. The boys didn't need to just camp out in front of the TV by themselves for hours, but she wasn't sure she was up for a game either. Then she got an idea.

"How about we pop some popcorn and watch a movie? What about Aladdin? That always makes us laugh. And I think we could use a lot of laughing today. What do you think?"

She couldn't stop her smile as the boys jumped up and down with excitement.

"Come on, Jordan. Let's go pick a stuffed animal to watch with us."

The boys hurried back upstairs, leaving Bailey and Nate alone.

Nate smiled, a hint of worry lingering in his eyes. "That's a great idea. If you three need time alone, I can hang out upstairs or even go for a long walk with Minnie."

"You should stay. If you want to, of course. No pressure, no judgment. Not everyone loves Disney movies."

He gave her an amused look. "I don't know. I think only monsters don't like Aladdin. I mean, I'd watch it for Robin Williams' genius if for no other reason." He slipped his hands into his pockets as his expression sobered. "I'm worried about you. Are you okay?"

She nodded, unwilling to talk about it now. "I will be." God willing.

She felt his eyes on her as she walked to the kitchen and started making the popcorn.

Ten minutes later, they each had a bowl, something to drink, and were settled in for the beginning of a movie that Bailey could easily quote from memory. The boys had set up on the floor with pillows and their stuffed animals, leaving the couch for the adults.

Bailey leaned into her corner, propped her feet on the coffee table and exhaled. For the first time all day, she felt completely relaxed. One minute, she was eating popcorn and watching the movie. The next, she was curled on her side on the couch, her head resting on her arm and a blanket draped over her shoulders. It took a moment to remember where she was and what was happening.

When she sat up, she saw that Nate had moved to the floor to sit with the boys, leaving her the couch to nap on.

How long had she been asleep?

A glance at the TV told her they were in the last fifteen minutes of the movie.

Nate spotted her and moved to join her on the couch again. "I hope you got some rest."

"I did, thank you. I obviously needed it. I don't even remember lying down."

"You've had a rough few days. Besides, I've enjoyed watching with the boys. I didn't realize how much more fun it is to watch movies like this with kids. Helps you see them in a whole new way, doesn't it?"

The movie ended, and Nate turned off the TV. Seth jumped up and ran over to the couch. "Wouldn't it be so cool to find a place full of treasure like the Cave of Wonders?"

Bailey chuckled. "Yes, it would. Very lucrative, too."

"Can we look for treasure tomorrow? Maybe there's more that we haven't found yet?"

"Look for treasure? Where?" Bailey prayed he was talking about Lego bricks or something similar, but worried he was referring to the old barn. If the latter were the case, she was about to squelch that idea. She really wished Seth didn't like the place so much.

"By the sunflower field where the lady found that watch. Maybe there's more."

"I forgot all about that." She sat up straight as all remnants of sleep disappeared. "I'm sure someone just dropped the watch near the field and then couldn't find it again. If there were a treasure, surely we would've noticed it by now."

Seth gave her a look of disbelief. "Then why didn't we see the watch before?"

He wasn't wrong.

"Maybe we can go out in a few days and take a look

around." She doubted they'd find anything, but it might be fun to go for a walk and look for treasures even if those treasures ended up being pretty rocks and discarded feathers. In the end, it would be a good adventure for the boys anyway, which was all that mattered.

That seemed to satisfy Seth. "Come on, Jordan. Let's go pretend we're treasure hunters."

They ran off together to play.

Nate looked curious. "Who found the watch? Do you still have it?"

"A customer brought it in. I intended to post something about it on social media, and then everything fell apart. It's in the drawer in the kitchen. I forgot all about it."

Chapter Twenty-Eight

Nate accepted the watch from Bailey and turned it over in his hand. They were sitting at the kitchen table where the lighting was good. He was no jewelry expert, but it was a Seiko and looked to be about mid-range. Someone probably spent at least a thousand dollars on it. He told Bailey as much.

"It's not in the best condition, is it?" It wasn't working, and there was mud caked in the creases of the band as well as the edging of the watch face. The band had come away from the watch face at one side, which was likely how it was lost in the first place. There was one light scratch across the glass there as well. "It's hard to know if it looks like this because it's old or because the elements did a number on it."

She nodded. "The lady who turned it in said she found it out by the sunflower field. I honestly don't know where out there, though. That covers a lot of area."

"Do you remember which day that was?"

"It was Saturday. I'm sure of it because that's the day I got the threatening letter."

Nate thought over the last week. "So there was no

significant weather right before that. Nothing that would've caused the dirt around the field to erode enough to reveal the watch. Although one could argue it might have taken years of that to finally unearth it." He rubbed a thumb over the watch face. "I'll bet the person who lost this was upset at the time."

"I imagine so. I was going to put up a vague post and insist that anyone who came in to claim it has to be able to describe it first. I was afraid posting a picture would bring in a lot of people hoping to snag it and resell it."

"Good thinking. No doubt you're right." He turned the watch over again. There was something on the back that looked like it might be more than just scratches. He pointed it out to Bailey. "Doesn't it look like it could be an inscription?"

She leaned in for a closer look. "It does. I can't make it out, though."

"Neither can I." He was interested in walking around the sunflower field like Seth suggested, although he doubted they'd find anything else.

He set the watch down on the table. "It might be worth taking it in to a jeweler and having it properly cleaned. If there *is* an inscription, it would help to be able to read it. I'm assuming if someone legitimately lost the watch, then that's the first thing they'll tell you to verify that it's theirs."

"That sounds like a good plan." She rested against the back of her kitchen chair. "Maybe I can take it in tomorrow at lunch. I figure we'll need a break from working on the store again."

Nate studied her for a moment and worked to keep his features neutral. "I took a gamble and set something up for tomorrow. Maybe I should've asked you first, but then it would've given you the opportunity to tell me no."

Her brows lifted, and she studied him as though she were trying to decide whether he was joking or not. "What did you do?"

He barked out a laugh. "Well, I might have brought it up originally, but it was a group effort." He paused for dramatic effect. "People from the police station, along with some family and friends, will be dropping by off and on all day tomorrow to help you power through cleaning up the store." He held up a hand. "And before you object, food is covered."

Bailey's mouth opened and closed again. She sat up straighter. "What?"

"People at the station know what's been happening around here, and they wanted to do something for you. So they're coming to help you. Dean from The Corner Café is donating sandwiches and chips for lunch. Tia is bringing pizza in for dinner. Your job is to tell people what you need them to do. Trust me, Bailey, everyone who's coming tomorrow is truly glad to have a way to help you through this."

She shook her head in disbelief as moisture filled her eyes. "I don't know what to say." She swallowed hard and swiped at a stray tear. "Thank you."

"You're welcome."

He hoped they'd be able to get a lot taken care of tomorrow. If they could clear out the rest of the trash and repair any displays that had been broken, then Bailey could start putting things back together again.

Hopefully, it'd take some pressure off her.

While Bailey went upstairs to get the boys ready for bed, Nate took Minnie out the back door for a walk. He stayed close by but paused near the back of the yard to play fetch with her for a few minutes.

By the vet's estimation, Minnie was around four years old, but he didn't think she'd ever outgrow the puppy stage. She was energy in motion, and he loved that about her. That extra energy was exactly what he needed to keep moving. Having a dog in your life meant having a friend who truly loved unconditionally. People sure could benefit from following that example.

Once Minnie was panting and she'd stopped sprinting after the ball, they headed back to the house. Nate was surprised to find Bailey sitting on the porch swing, a book in her hands. She looked up and smiled.

"Looks like you wore Minnie out."

"Until tomorrow." Nate chuckled. He let Minnie into the house so she could get a drink of water and rest. "Do you mind if I join you?"

"Not at all." She scooted down a little to give him plenty of room. The swing shifted with his weight then settled into a gentle back-and-forth motion.

She set the book on a small wooden table beside the swing. That's when Nate could see what it was.

"That's a beautiful Bible."

Bailey wrapped a hand around one of the chains that held up the swing. "Thank you. I've had several, but this is my favorite. My youth pastor gave it to me after I was baptized. I used to spend time reading after the boys went to bed, but I've fallen out of the habit. I figured it was time to start doing that again."

"It's a good habit to have. I usually do the same after I feed Minnie and while I'm eating breakfast." They sat in comfortable silence for several moments before he asked, "Did the boys go to bed okay?"

"They were both tired. They didn't protest. Much." She chuckled. "I'd think they were sick if they didn't try to extend bedtime at least a little every night."

More silence. Nate wanted to ask her what she and Jenny talked about earlier but didn't want to pry or make Bailey feel uncomfortable. He was about to bring up the plan for tomorrow when she pulled one knee up and clasped her hands around it.

She took in a deep breath. "I can't lose you, Nate."

"What?" He shifted so he could see her better. "Why would you lose me?"

She seemed to focus on a spot on her knee as she considered her words. "Our friendship. It means a lot to me. I'm afraid of losing that if things don't..." She swallowed hard and shook her head. "I'm sorry. I'm making a mess of this."

Nate needed her to finish that sentence. "If things don't what?"

"If things changed between us and... didn't work out." Her lashes lifted as she swung her gaze to him.

He could relate to the uncertainty he saw there, but it was the hope that had his heart pounding against his ribs. "That's impossible." He spoke the words with such conviction that her eyes widened in surprise.

"How can you possibly know that for sure?"

There were a lot of things in this world that had him second-guessing what was right or not. But his feelings for Bailey? They were never in question. His only worry was whether or not she could ever feel the same way.

Chapter Twenty-Nine

The look in Nate's eyes was intense as he studied her. Bailey held her breath, uncertain what he was about to say. He seemed so sure that, no matter what, he would always be there for her. He couldn't understand how much his friendship meant to her. Right now, she was walking a tightrope between the stability of keeping him as just a friend and the uncertainty of admitting that she cared for him as more than that.

He leaned forward a little. "Bailey, I've been in love with you for years."

She hadn't been sure what she expected him to say, but that wasn't it. She opened her mouth to respond and closed it again. "You wha—? How is that—? But you never..."

Nate ran a hand over his face and stood abruptly, the swing swaying back and forth unevenly. He paced to the railing around the porch, paused there, and then turned to face her again.

"I pretty much fell for you the first time we met. Then you and Joe hit it off, and there was no stopping what was between you. I wouldn't have wanted to because it was obvious you were made for each other." He raked a hand through his hair. "I was genuinely happy for you both. Please believe me on that. You were two of my best friends, and I wasn't going to jeopardize that. Jeopardize your happiness together."

"I know you wouldn't." Bailey used her foot to stop the swing's movement. "I had no idea." Her words came out barely above a whisper.

"Which is exactly the way it was supposed to stay."

Until now. Until a wrench was thrown into the machine of life, and circumstances changed.

The reality of what Nate was saying burrowed into Bailey's chest. To keep a secret like that for over eight years... She couldn't even imagine.

Nate leaned against the railing, his hands gripping the edge. "I've prayed for these feelings to disappear—to fall in love with someone else. But no matter how much time passed... It was always you." He groaned. "Joe was like a brother to me. Even now, I feel like I'm betraying him just by saying all of this out loud. The last thing I want to do is hurt you or Seth or Jordan. Bailey, I worry about losing you, too. It would *kill* me." The truth of his words was written on his face as his eyes found hers.

She stood slowly, suddenly aware of the pressure of her feet against the wooden planks beneath them—of the humidity in the air and the crickets chirping in the fading sunlight.

But most of all, she was aware of the magnetic pull she felt toward Nate. A pull that wouldn't go away no matter how much she tried to focus on the scary unknowns in the future. "You can't lose me either."

Nate pushed away from the railing and took several

steps forward, stopping an arm's length away. "How can you be so sure?"

She stepped forward then, the tips of her shoes touching his. She tipped her chin up so that she could see his face. "Because I'm falling in love with you too."

With one strong arm, he tugged her close and leaned in to kiss her, his other hand cupping her jaw. The kiss was intense as their worries and fears collided with the relief and adrenaline of knowing that they felt the same way.

Nate broke the kiss long enough to smile at her. With a hand resting against the back of his neck, she smiled back and then gently tugged him close again.

This time, when they kissed, it was sweet and slow. He pressed his lips against her cheek, another by her earlobe, and then pulled her into a hug.

Bailey rested her cheek against his chest and listened as his heart thrummed in her ear. She wasn't sure how long they stood there before his phone started to ring. He kissed her forehead and withdrew the phone from a back pocket. He looked down at her with a sparkle in his eyes as he answered.

"This is Nate." He paused as he listened. "Hold on, Paris. I'm going to put you on speaker so Bailey can hear you, too." He hit a button. "Okay, you're good."

"Good evening, Bailey."

"Hey, Detective. You're working late tonight."

"More often than not. The only reason I get away with it is because Eve works just as much." He chuckled. "I wanted to pass along some information. First of all, the lab dusted the cardboard box that was left in front of your property for prints. There were none other than Bailey's. No surprise given the lack of fingerprints on evidence collected previously."

Nate motioned toward the house, and Bailey nodded. They went back inside and took a seat at the kitchen table, the cell phone lying in front of them as Detective Paris continued.

"We spoke to animal control. They were young Western diamondback rattlesnakes. Unfortunately, they could've been caught in the wild in any number of places nearby."

So far, there wasn't much in the way of encouraging news. Bailey fought to not let it get her down. There had to be a way to find this guy. To track him down and stop him before he did something else to harm her family.

Nate reached over and took her hand in his before speaking. "We were hoping the team would be able to get more info than that."

"Me, too. But we did find some information that might be helpful. Logan dug into the history of your property, Bailey. He's here now. I'm going to turn the call over to him."

Nate quickly hit the mute button. "Logan Alcott is our IT guy. If information exists somewhere, he has a way of finding it." He took the call off mute. He still held Bailey's hand, running his thumb over the back of hers.

"Hey, guys. So, it took a little digging, but I found some interesting tidbits. Your farm was owned by the same family for years until you and Joe bought it. Adam Tinsley inherited it from his parents when they passed in the late nineties. Adam and his wife, Cici, had a large estate built along with the barn that's there now. Apparently, there were living quarters on the top floor of the barn for hired help to stay on the property."

Bailey tried to picture it in her mind. "Wow, sounds like the barn was quite impressive back in the day. What kind of livestock did they have that warranted such a fancy setup?"

"They considered raising thoroughbreds, and that's what it was designed for. However, they never did pursue it. Adam and Cici had one child. A daughter named Sophia. She was in and out of trouble a lot. Her parents reported her missing two separate times, only to have her show back up a few days later. According to the reports, it wasn't unusual for her to sneak out of the house or run away after an argument with her parents."

Bailey felt for the girl's parents. Her boys were still young, but the idea that either of them would sneak out of the house at night or disappear without telling her where they were going sounded like an absolute nightmare.

There was some shuffling in the background as Logan continued. "At some point, things started to fall apart between Mr. and Mrs. Tinsley. She filed for divorce in 2012 and walked away with half of everything in the bank account, but he kept the house and property."

"What happened with the daughter?" Nate went to the fridge and motioned to it, asking Bailey if she wanted something to drink. She nodded, and he brought back a bottle of water for each of them before sitting down again.

"Sophia stayed here with her father. There were no custody papers drawn up that I could find. She was seventeen at the time."

"The whole situation sounds terribly sad." Bailey frowned.

"It gets worse. A year after her parents divorced, Sophia disappeared again, and her father filed a missing person's report. Sophia was eighteen by then, and while an investigation was opened, there was no evidence to support foul play. She was deemed a runaway, and that was that. Six months later, the house went up in flames. Mr. Tinsley escaped in time, but the house was a total loss. An extensive investigation was conducted, and it was later determined that faulty wiring in the basement led to the fire."

Nate shook his head sadly. "Poor guy was put through the wringer, wasn't he?"

"He eventually had the debris removed and then built the house that you currently live in. He finally decided to sell the place, and that's when you and Joe purchased the property."

Bailey wished she'd known all of this when they bought the place. They'd gone through the real estate company and never met the owner. It was possible Adam Tinsley wasn't even in town at that time.

She took a sip of her water and replaced the cap. "Do we know where he is now? Is it possible he's the one trying to get us to sell because he regrets the decision in the first place?"

Detective Paris's voice came back on the line. "We're trying to locate him. I'd like to have a conversation and ask him some specific questions as to how other buyers might have approached him. There might be something—or someone—that connects to the trouble you've been having, Bailey."

"We've got another small puzzle we're working on over here, too." Nate told them about the watch. "I'm taking it in to be cleaned tomorrow. There's a good chance someone who visited Bailey's business dropped it at some point, but it's definitely worth pursuing."

"Excellent. Keep me updated on what you find. If you end up with a name or initials, Logan can run a search and compare that with anyone associated with the property just in case there's a match."

Logan's voice came through from the background. "Just say the word."

The conversation ended, leaving Nate and Bailey at the table, absorbing the information. There were still way more questions than they had answers, but for the first time, she felt like that might change soon.

Chapter Thirty

I t felt surreal to see Bailey the next morning and be able to greet her with a kiss. She'd blushed, and Nate had enjoyed every moment of it before the morning was moving forward at full speed. Bailey got the boys dressed and fed while Nate took care of Minnie and washed the dishes. Then, they checked on and fed the goats and ducks on their way to the store. People started showing up to help at eight. Nate had opened the front gate so they could come and go as needed.

He was worried that Bailey might feel overwhelmed. She hadn't seen a lot of the people coming in to help since Joe's funeral, and there were many she'd never met. She quickly proved that she was on top of things and a skilled delegator.

Rachel was there, as well as Jenny. Both women promised to help Bailey keep an eye on Seth and Jordan.

Originally, Nate planned to take at least Jordan and maybe Seth to help him drop the watch off at the jewelry store. He was getting ready to talk to Bailey about it when

Detective Paris came in. He looked around at the bustling store and nodded his approval before zeroing in on Nate.

"Walker." They shook hands. "Logan located Adam Tinsley. He moved some years ago to this side of Austin. He was reluctant to speak over the phone, so I'm heading that way now to question him. I thought you might want to come along."

Nate tried to keep the surprise from his face. He wanted the opportunity to hear what Tinsley had to say, and Austin was just over an hour away. He would've refused to leave Bailey except that she and her sons were surrounded by some of the people he trusted the most.

Paris must have anticipated his worry because he nodded toward Jenny. "I've asked Durant to stay until we get back regardless of whether anyone else gets called out."

"That sounds great. Do you mind if we drop the watch off at the jewelry store for cleaning on the way out of town?"

"Not a problem. See you out front in five."

Nate found Bailey at the back of the store, took her aside, and told her where he and Paris were going. "At the very least, Jenny will be here with you. Most likely, you'll be surrounded by officers all day. You and the boys will be safe. But don't hesitate to call if you need me. Okay?"

She nodded. "I really hope you guys get some information we can use."

"So do I. Stay safe." He gave her hand a squeeze when he really wanted to kiss her goodbye. "I'll text you when we're on our way back."

"Be careful?"

"Always."

He knew Bailey, Seth, and Jordan were going to be

okay. If their suspect had any sense of self-preservation, he'd steer clear of the property today.

⁂

Driving into Austin was a good reminder of why Nate preferred to live in a smaller town like Destiny. Sure, there were upsides to living in a big city: more places to shop, a wider range of medical care, and more job opportunities.

But it also meant more traffic and pollution, not to mention the sheer number of people. Policing in a city like this would be a whole different ballgame.

Paris had put Tinsley's address into GPS and followed directions until they arrived at a single-story home in a newer, wealthy neighborhood. While Tinsley's house wasn't huge, it certainly fit right in with those around it. A large circular drive was surrounded by a perfectly mani-cured lawn and flower beds that left a serious impression. Nate imagined they must look amazing in the spring when the flowers were blooming.

They drove partway around the circular drive and parked in front of the sidewalk that led to the front door.

The men got out and approached the home. The front door was easily ten feet high and solid wood with metal work along the edges and across the top.

Paris rang the doorbell and looked right into the camera situated above it. "Detective John Paris here to speak with Mr. Adam Tinsley." He lifted his badge.

A few minutes later, they could hear someone unlocking the door before opening it wide.

A heavy-set man in a wheelchair greeted them with an extended hand. "Adam. Good to meet you." His gaze swung to Nate.

"You as well." Paris introduced Nate, and they followed Tinsley inside.

The interior of the house was as nice as it looked on the outside, if not more so. The open floor plan and large windows made it one of the brightest homes Nate had ever been in. It was clear that Tinsley spared no expense when he had it built.

Even if he technically downgraded from the large home and property in Destiny, he didn't skimp on quality.

"You have a lovely home," Nate told him as they followed him into a large living room with vaulted ceilings.

"Thank you. Can I offer either of you some water or coffee?"

Paris held up a hand. "No, but thank you."

"No thanks." Nate took a seat on the leather sectional. By the cleanliness of everything, Nate was willing to bet Tinsley didn't own a pet.

The other man wheeled up next to the recliner and studied his guests. From their background information, Nate knew the man was in his late sixties. The plethora of wrinkles on his weathered face, signs of exhaustion, and white hair made him look much older than his years. Nate supposed going through what he had would definitely age a man.

Tinsley folded his hands and rested them on his lap. "You mentioned that you had questions for me regarding the property I sold in Destiny a few years ago. You'll forgive me if I ask directly whether it has anything to do with my daughter."

"I'm afraid it doesn't. I was very sorry to hear that she's missing." Paris leaned forward from his spot on the couch. "The people who purchased your property have been having some trouble lately. Much of the harassment seems to center around trying to get them to sell the place. Did you have any similar trouble before you moved?"

Tinsley looked thoughtful as he mulled over the question. "There was always the occasional realtor who came with a supposed offer from a buyer—maybe a couple of times a year. I wasn't interested, so I never asked to hear more. Now, once I decided to sell, they all came out of the woodwork. Most of them were investors who wanted to snatch up the land and turn it into plots or build apartment buildings. I just knew my parents would roll over in their graves if I knowingly allowed that to happen."

"Which is why you eventually sold it to the couple."

Tinsley's eyes lit up. "It was my hope that they'd enjoy living there, raise a family, and maybe even pass it on to their kids one day." His expression sobered. "I'd hoped to do that myself, but my daughter never cared to live there anyway. She hated Destiny and dreamed of moving to a big city someday. Then, when she disappeared, I didn't have anyone to pass it along to. I wanted to have some control over who I sold it to while I could."

It made sense. Then, no matter what Joe and Bailey might have chosen to do with the property, at least Tinsley felt like he did his best to keep the land the way his parents might have wanted. Nate could certainly admire the effort.

He leaned forward. "Did you ever have problems with people trespassing on the property?"

"Once caught a man out there trying to hunt on the back acres. He was arrested for trespassing and illegal hunting. Other than that, there was the occasional camping site I found after the fact where they'd obviously set up a campfire. Twice, I had to break up a bunch of teenagers throwing a party, but it wasn't a big deal." Tinsley frowned, the lines at the corners of his eyes and mouth deepening. "If there was a group of teens causing trouble, my Sophia was usually involved. I never understood why she was so unhappy with her life, but there was nothing her mother or I could do to make her content."

Nate could only imagine the heartbreak of seeing your child drift away and being unable to stop it. "I'm sorry, sir, for all you've gone through. To not know where she is or what happened to her must be incredibly difficult."

Tinsley gripped the arms of his wheelchair and straightened his spine. "My daughter didn't run away. Not like it states in her report. She was murdered, and I'm certain it was that no good boyfriend of hers who did it."

Chapter Thirty-One

Detective Paris leaned forward. "I didn't see anything about that in any of the police reports. Did you ever express your concern about foul play?"

Tinsley flinched. "I told the officers at the time, but they figured I was reaching for answers. They weren't wrong. Sophia ran away from home multiple times. The longest she stayed away was five days before she came back. I always reported her missing, and there was a part of me that worried she wouldn't return." He swallowed hard, his Adam's apple bobbing. "I couldn't blame them for assuming she'd run away that time, too. I kept hoping that was the case because maybe it'd mean she'd eventually come to her senses and would return home."

There was silence as what the older man said settled over them all.

Nate cleared his throat, the sound loud compared to the quiet room. "Why do you think her boyfriend might be responsible for her disappearance?"

Tinsley took a deep breath as though he were trying to

gather his thoughts. "They were together off and on for about a year. Sophia never told me how old he was, but I suspected he was several years older than her. Now, don't get me wrong, my daughter made plenty of poor decisions. But it was often Jeremy who either suggested them in the first place or organized them. She liked the bad boys." He shook his head sadly. "About two weeks before she disappeared, she found out that he'd been cheating on her. I don't know with who. Though drugs and alcohol and petty thefts didn't seem to bother her, cheating was where she drew the line. She left him."

Good for her.

"He wouldn't accept it. Kept coming around. Calling. Begging. Sending flowers. I found him on my property twice, trying to get her attention by throwing things at her bedroom window. He swore they were meant to be together." His eyes grew moist, and he swiped a tear away with one knuckle of his weathered hand. "One night, she snuck out and went to a party that I later learned was on my property. Her friends said she was there, and then at one point they couldn't find her. That was the last time anyone saw my daughter."

Paris leaned back and wrote several things on his phone. "Did you ever see Jeremy again? Did he ever ask about Sophia?"

"I never saw him again. Mutual friends said he moved to be closer to where his father lived, but I never even knew his father's name. I tried to locate Jeremy and never could, and no one had a clue. It's like he vanished right along with Sophia."

The detective nodded as he made some more notes. "Do you remember Jeremy's last name?"

"Price." There was no hesitation in the answer. "He

lived over on Cherry Street, or at least that's what Sophia told me at the time. I never knew what to believe, though."

"I appreciate your patience. I'm sure it's not easy going through all this again." Paris slid his phone into his pocket. "I did want to ask one more question. Why did you decide to sell the property in Destiny?"

"I had to try and move on with my life. I stayed for five years after she disappeared, and every day, I waited and hoped she would return. I didn't want to leave because I worried that she'd come home, and I'd miss her. It was debilitating. I just knew that I had to put some distance between myself and that house. Too many memories. You know?"

Nate had to give the guy a lot of credit. It'd be hard not to continue to hold out hope that your loved one would return.

Paris pulled out a business card. "If you think of anything else, or if someone were to contact you about the property in Destiny, I'd appreciate it if you gave me a call. I'm going to be honest. The case we're investigating currently likely has nothing to do with you or your daughter, but I like to be thorough. If I find anything related to Sophia or Jeremy Price, I'll be in touch."

"Thank you. That's all I can ask for." Tinsley reached out to shake both of their hands. "If you have any other questions for me, feel free to call. I know it's a bit of a drive, but you're welcome to drop by if you'd prefer. I'd just appreciate some heads-up. Sometimes, it can take a bit of time and effort to get to the door." He slapped the armrests of his wheelchair good-naturedly.

"Absolutely. Thank you again, sir."

Nate and Paris got into the car and continued down the curved driveway and onto the road out front.

Paris glanced over at Nate. "First impressions?"

"He seemed genuine. I didn't feel like he was hiding anything. It seems possible that his daughter and the boyfriend might have run off together and simply never looked back. Especially since Mr. Tinsley couldn't locate Jeremy after the fact." He couldn't imagine doing that to someone who cared about him, but then it was impossible to know the mental health of the young woman. There could've been a lot of factors at play that they had no knowledge of.

"I had similar thoughts." Paris tapped the steering wheel with both thumbs. "I'd like to know more about this Jeremy Price. I want to interview him if he's still in the area somewhere. Assuming Mr. Tinsley was truthful about Jeremy stalking his daughter and trespassing to get to her, the similarities shouldn't be ignored."

He dialed Logan's number over the speaker. When the tech answered, Paris told him what they knew about Jeremy Price as well as Sophia Tinsley. "See if you can figure out what happened to Jeremy and if he's still living in the area. Expand out from there if needed. If they did run off together, it's doubtful they had the funds to live on their own. Chances are, they're in the system somewhere."

"Will do. Want me to call with results?"

"We're headed to Destiny now. Should be back in an hour and a half. I'll find you at the station."

"Yes, sir."

The call ended at the same time Nate's cell phone pinged. He glanced at the incoming text. "Looks like the watch is cleaned and ready to be picked up." When they dropped it off, Paris had gone inside as well. They'd let the jeweler know that it could be connected to a case they were investigating, and the jeweler assured them he would move the watch to the top of his list.

"Perfect. We'll swing by and pick it up before I drop you back off at the farm. If Logan finds anything, I'll give you and Bailey a call."

"I appreciate that." Nate hoped that all of this would lead to some concrete answers soon. For now, he couldn't wait to get back to Bailey and the kids.

Chapter Thirty-Two

Bailey was exhausted, but it was the good kind of tired that came with knocking a ton of things off her to-do list. People were still at the store, helping by hauling trash out, sweeping, and dusting. A couple of guys from the station even repaired several shelves. It was seriously an answer to prayer.

Seth and Jordan seemed to thrive on having so many people around. Bailey didn't know what she would've done if it hadn't been for Jenny and Rachel keeping an eye on them. When Bailey had to focus on specific tasks, the other two women stepped in to keep the boys entertained.

Dean delivered the fresh sandwiches from his cafe himself, and everyone happily devoured the delicious lunch.

If things kept progressing like this through the after-noon, they should have no problem getting the store clean enough to open to the public on Friday. It'd take time to restock products, but at least what they did have would be available along with the pumpkins, gourds, and sunflowers.

Bailey checked her phone for what might have been the

hundredth time, hoping for an update from Nate. She knew he was busy and riding along with Detective Paris, but after spending so much time together the last few days, it was weird not to have him there now.

She missed him, especially after their conversation and kisses last night. Just thinking about it made her face warm. She still couldn't get over the fact that Nate had loved her for over eight years. She could never accuse him of not being able to keep a secret.

The thought coaxed a smile onto her face just in time for Jenny to notice. She and Jordan were busy moving bars of soap from a cardboard box back onto the newly-repaired shelf. Jenny waved her over.

Bailey spotted Seth helping Rachel organize things on the main counter and made her way toward her friend.

Jenny handed a bar of green soap to Jordan, but her attention was on Bailey. "Judging from that smile and the way you can't stop checking your phone, am I correct in assuming that things are going well between you and a certain individual you wish were here?" She waggled her brows.

There were far too many people within earshot to go into details. Instead, Bailey beamed and shrugged. "Maybe."

With a triumphant grin, Jenny stood and gave Bailey a hug. "I'm so happy to hear that."

"Mommy, look." Jordan waved at the shelf of colorful soaps as though he were revealing a piece of art in a museum. "They look neat!"

"Yes, they do. Great job, sweetie." Bailey got down to his level and gave him a big hug. "We couldn't have done this without you." She winked at Jenny over the top of his head and stood up.

Jenny nudged her in the side. "Hey, looks like Nate's back. I hope he and Paris were able to get something useful. I half expected the suspect to show up here today. Kinda wish he had. Talk about walking into a lion's den." She laughed. "Go on, see what they found. Jordan and I are going to move on to the lotions next, aren't we?"

Jordan stood tall, crossed his arms in front of him, and gave a definitive nod.

Bailey spotted Nate toward the front of the store. As soon as their gazes locked, her heart rate sped up. He picked his way through the volunteers until he reached her. "Hey, you."

"You're back." She smiled up at him and lowered her voice. "I missed you."

"I missed you, too." He motioned toward the front door of the store. "Can you step outside with me for a few minutes?" He took a watch from his pocket and held it out to her. "I thought you might want to look at this now that it's been cleaned. I also wanted to tell you about the meeting with Mr. Tinsley."

Bailey knew Jenny had Jordan. She scanned the room and spotted Rachel who looked up from her place with Seth, noticed them, and gave a wave.

"Sure, that would be great." She followed him through the store and into the fresh air outside.

They sat beside each other at one of the picnic tables.

Bailey turned the watch over in her hand and marveled at how shiny it was. "Wow, you'll have to tell me which jewelry store you took this to. This is seriously impressive."

"I went ahead and had the jeweler fix the band. He said the pin had been bent horribly and that the watch had likely been forcibly removed from the wrist, whether purposefully or not."

"Well, they did a beautiful job. It hardly looks like the same watch."

"I wouldn't have believed it if it weren't for the inscription on the back. It's faded, but you can read it now that the dirt and grime are gone." Nate placed an elbow on the table that Bailey was leaning against, his wrist resting against her arm.

She brought the watch closer and had to squint a little to read the words.

"A father's love never fades. - Dad."

Nate scratched his chin. "We took photos of the watch along with the inscription and gave them to Logan at the precinct." He went on to tell her about the conversation with Mr. Tinsley and what he'd said about his daughter and her boyfriend.

Bailey's heart ached for the man. "That's all so sad. Do you think there's anything to his concerns?"

"He was pretty convincing. Logan's trying to track down the boyfriend this afternoon. I don't know if there's any connection between him and the trouble you've been having, but if we can offer the poor father any closure at all, it'll be worth it."

Nate lightly rubbed her arm with his thumb. "I thought about you all morning. Couldn't wait to get back. Has it been a good day?"

She leaned into his arm a little as she told him about all the people who had come by to help out. Most only stayed an hour or two, but there were enough volunteers to keep repairs and cleaning moving forward.

"I wish there was a way that I could really thank everyone for what they're doing. I was thinking about opening for an extra evening and inviting them all to come by. Maybe cook hot dogs and let people pick out a pumpkin to keep if they want to. What do you think?"

"I think it's a great idea and very sweet of you to want to do that." He glanced at her hair. A section had fallen from her bun, and he gently curled it around his finger.

"I know. My hair is a mess." She patted her head and finally released the bun. After gathering her hair again and smoothing it down, she twisted it back into place before securing it. When she'd finished, she found Nate watching her intently.

"You are so beautiful, Bailey. Inside and out."

His words were said in a whisper, but they settled over her heart. She ducked her chin as a blush crept into her cheeks. "You're sweet."

The front of the store opened, and Jenny poked her head out. "Hey, Bailey, Carl finished building the new shelves and needs to know where you want them." She gave them an apologetic look followed by an amused smile before disappearing back into the store.

Nate stood reluctantly. "I'm going to run back to your house and check on Minnie. I'm sure she's ready for a chance to run outside for a bit. Do you want me to take the boys? They might enjoy the change of scenery. No pressure, though."

"That's a great idea. I'm sure Rachel and Jenny could use the break." She chuckled. "I'll be right back."

Inside, she told her friends the plan. The boys were thrilled with the idea of going back to the house with Nate.

"Make sure you listen to Nate and don't cause trouble." She gave them her best stern look.

"Yes, ma'am," they echoed.

She gave them each a hug, ignoring her instinct to give Nate one, too. They hadn't had a chance to talk about it yet, but she wanted to keep this new change in their relationship on the down-low until things settled a little. "You boys give Minnie a pat for me."

"We won't be gone too long." Nate held up the watch. "And I'll put this in a safe place for now. If Logan doesn't find anything significant, you should be free to post something on social media next week."

"Sounds like a plan." Bailey waved goodbye and watched them drive away before finally turning to go inside. She answered questions about the shelves and then found Jenny and Rachel chatting in the office area. She walked in and gave them both a hug. "You two are seriously my heroes today. I owe you both a steak dinner or spa day or something. Without kids, of course."

Both women assured her that they didn't mind hanging out with her sons one bit.

"Seth kept things interesting," Rachel said with a smile. "He mentioned the watch and how you guys are going to go treasure hunting by the sunflowers. He has such a great imagination."

"Yes, he does. I told him we could go walking around the field but not to expect to find much. Nate took the watch in to have it cleaned, and it has an inscription on the back." She recited it for them. "I'll put up a general post on social media next week and see if anyone contacts us."

"That's a good idea." Jenny leaned against the small desk in one corner of the little space. "Someone must have missed it at some point."

Rachel nodded. "I'm sure that's true. Why wait until next week? If you post it before Friday, someone might come in while we're open to ask about it."

"Someone at the precinct is looking into several leads, and he's cross-referencing the watch just in case. I doubt there's any connection between it and the guy who's been harassing us, but you never know what may turn up. Maybe someone reported it missing at some point, especially since it's a more expensive watch and clearly has sentimental value." Bailey shrugged. "Either way, I hope we can find the owner."

A knock at the open door drew the ladies' attention to Officer Clint Baker. "Hey, Bailey. Nate mentioned you were looking for a company to take down that old barn. My brother, Drew, is a demolition contractor who will be happy to give you a free estimate. Tell him I sent you, and he'll take good care of you guys." He handed her a business card.

"This is perfect, Clint, thank you. I'll give him a call first thing tomorrow." She flashed him a smile. She'd rather call someone a friend recommended than go with a company she knew nothing about. As far as she was concerned, it was a bonus that this was Clint's brother.

"Not a problem." He gave a wave and went back into the main part of the store.

Bailey read the business card and slid it into her back pocket with a happy sigh. Today was full of a lot of positives. Just the support she'd seen from friends was enough to remind her that, no matter how bad things might look, brighter days were coming. Things were starting to come together. Now she prayed they would catch the man responsible for all this mess before he struck again.

Chapter Thirty-Three

Nate lost track of how many people he shook hands with. Pizza had been consumed, all the volunteers thanked, and the store looked amazing. Now it was just him and Bailey, Rachel, Jenny, and the kids, and everyone was exhausted.

Rachel took in the building with satisfaction. "I've got to say, people came through in a big way. We should be able to open normally on Friday."

"It's truly a miracle." Bailey collapsed on a stool behind the main counter. "Tomorrow evening, I'll focus on getting some pumpkins lined up out front for those who don't want to go down to pick them directly from the vines."

"I'm happy to help." Nate flashed her a smile.

"I appreciate that." When Bailey returned the smile, there was an added warmth to it. He couldn't wait to sneak a kiss in later.

Jenny stretched and hopped up to sit on the counter. "I'm looking forward to a long bath, some chocolate, and a good night's sleep."

Bailey pointed to her. "Amen, sister."

Nate's phone rang, and Paris's name flashed on the screen.

He answered it immediately. "This is Nate."

"Hey. I'm here with Logan. We've been able to dig up some more information."

"Great. Let me put this on speaker." Nate did so and set the phone down.

Bailey glanced at Seth, who was watching them curiously. "I'm going to take the boys out to play." It was clear she didn't want them to overhear any details.

"Oh! Let me do that." Rachel held out a hand to each of the brothers. "Come on, boys. Did I see some dominoes in that toy chest out there? Let's see if we can build a long chain of dominoes and then knock them down."

"Are you sure?" Bailey hopped down from the stool. "We're good if you want to head home."

"Don't you worry. I've got this." With a wink and a smile, she led the boys over to the toy chest.

Nate moved into the small office where the three of them gathered around the desk. He set the phone down and put it on speaker. "All right, Paris. You've got me, Jenny, and Bailey here." He put a hand against Bailey's lower back, and she immediately leaned into the touch.

"Hey, guys," Logan said. "Mr. Tinsley mentioned that Jeremy Price lived on Cherry Street, so I started my search there. No one with the last name Price has ever lived on Cherry Street in Destiny. There was also never a Jeremy Price registered with the Destiny School District."

Paris spoke up. "Since Mr. Tinsley said Jeremy seemed several years older than Sophia, he may not have attended school in the area. I got the impression they probably met at one of the parties Sophia liked to sneak off to."

"That's what I was thinking, too," Logan agreed. "So I

expanded the search to all school districts in Texas, and I found a Jeremy Price registered in Denton County. His file there was filled with all kinds of behavioral issues. He was suspended twice for inappropriate behavior and fighting. It looks like he lived with his father at the time, a Warren Price. After the last suspension, he dropped out of school and never went back."

Paris cleared his throat. "I reached out to law enforcement in Denton. Jeremy was questioned about a number of petty thefts and property damage reports, but somehow he always managed to skate by due to lack of evidence. He was never booked into the system. I've got a call into Warren Price, but he hasn't returned it yet. Logan did find photos of him from the school district in Denton. We sent a copy over to Mr. Tinsley, and he verified that he's the same guy that Sophia was dating."

"Then we can assume Jeremy left Denton after he dropped out of school and came here to Destiny. But why Destiny?" Bailey reached up and scratched behind her right ear. "I mean, I love our community, don't get me wrong, but why would you just randomly choose this place as your destination?"

"Something must have brought him here," Jenny agreed. "So we know Jeremy had issues with violence and inappropriate behavior before he moved to Destiny. We have confirmation that he's the one who was seeing Sophia Tinsley. Have you been able to figure out where Jeremy is now?"

"That's the weird part," Logan said over the phone. "It's like the guy just disappeared after that. No online activity or any bank accounts opened under his name. However, there is one more thing we found. Detective?"

There was some clattering in the background before

Paris's voice joined the conversation again. "I sent a photo of the watch that was found on the property over to Mr. Tinsley. He not only identified it as his daughter's watch but was able to tell me the inscription word for word. He said he bought it for her when she started to pull away from him because he wanted it to be a reminder that, no matter what happened, he loved her, and she could always come back home. She wore it all the time, and when she took it off to go to bed, she placed it in a dish on her side table. He's certain she was wearing it the night she disappeared because he hadn't been able to find it since."

Nate couldn't ignore the sinking feeling in the pit of his stomach. "The jeweler said that it would have taken some force to break the band." Had Sophia and Jeremy argued? Did he grab her arm, and that's how the band was broken? Maybe Mr. Tinsley's worry about his daughter being murdered wasn't so over the top. "I hate to ask this, Logan, but have you done a search for Jane Does in Texas to see if any match Sophia's description?"

"I did, and there were no matches. Plus, Sophia had been brought in by police several times for petty theft and once with a group of teens after a large party was broken up. Her fingerprints are in the system. Even if her body had turned up somewhere else, they should've been able to identify her—"

Paris's voice broke in. "I'm getting a call from Warren Price. I'll be back in a few minutes."

Bailey shivered. "What if Sophia was killed right here on this property?"

Nate slid his hand from her lower back to her shoulder and gave it a reassuring clasp. "Even if that were true, then what happened to Jeremy?"

They talked about several possibilities while they

waited for the detective to return. The sound of a door opening and shutting signaled that he'd re-joined Logan.

"All right, I spoke with Mr. Price. He said that his son took off after he dropped out of high school. Since Jeremy was almost eighteen at the time, the father wasn't worried about it and, frankly, he was relieved to no longer be stressed about what his son was going to do next."

"Wow." Bailey shook her head. "I can't even imagine."

Price quickly continued. "I asked if he knew why Jeremy might have come to Destiny. It turns out that his mother lived here, and Jeremy often threatened his father with changing his last name to hers. I got the impression Warren would've been just fine with that. If that's the case, we need to be looking for a Jeremy Carmichael."

"Carmichael?" Why did the name sound familiar to Nate?

Bailey's form stiffened as she straightened. "What was his mother's name?"

"Rachel Carmichael."

Chapter Thirty-Four

The moment Nate heard the name Rachel Carmichael, he snatched up his phone. "Rachel works here with Bailey." He spun around and strode to the door of the office. "Seth? Jordan?" His boots echoed through the room as he crossed the floor to the small table and toy box. Dominoes had been taken out and a line started, but the young boys were nowhere to be seen.

Bailey reached out and gripped his arm. "Maybe she took them outside to play cornhole." Her voice wavered with doubt and fear.

Nate grasped her hand in his, and they jogged to the front door to look outside. There was no sign of them, and Rachel's car was gone.

Bailey pulled her phone out. "I'm going to try and call her." She stepped away as she put the phone to her ear.

Paris's voice came over the speaker. "Walker. Update."

"It looks like Rachel took Seth and Jordan. Her car isn't out front. There's a good chance she was listening in on the conversation." Nate's stomach clenched. Seth and Jordan trusted Rachel, they'd have no reason to doubt her if she told them to go with her somewhere. He prayed that the time Rachel spent with the boys meant she cared too much to harm them. "We need to send someone to her place right now."

Bailey turned and shook her head. "She's not answering her phone." She relayed Rachel's address and a description of her car.

They could hear typing on a keyboard before Logan spoke. "I've verified her address, and I have the license plate number now."

Paris spoke into the phone. "We're putting a BOLO out on her car. I'm sending officers to her address. Logan, find out where Jeremy lives."

"Yes, sir. I'm on it."

Jenny was writing everything down as well.

Meanwhile, Bailey stood staring at the little table and chairs where the boys should have been playing. "How could Rachel get to know the boys and spend time with them for nearly two years and then just take them away from me? How did I not know?"

Nate sidestepped into her line of sight. "Don't do that. Don't start questioning yourself. You need to stay focused. We're going to find Seth and Jordan." He placed a finger beneath her chin and raised it until her eyes were on him. "I've seen her interact with them, and she cares about them. I refuse to believe she'd do anything to hurt them."

Bailey sniffed and gave a small nod. "Yeah. I can't imagine that, either."

All Nate could figure at this point was that Rachel was acting to protect her son. Whether she knew about his actions or not, that instinct to be there for him remained.

"Okay," Logan began. "Jeremy lives on the other side of town. He's married to a woman named Rose. Looks like they got married about two years after Sophia went missing. They have three young children. As Jeremy Carmichael, his record is spotless. Not so much as a parking ticket." He spouted off the home address as well as the car Jeremy drove so they could be on the lookout for it, too.

"Officers are on the way to Jeremy's house," Paris announced.

"What about us?" Bailey asked, her eyes wide. "Nate, we have to look for them. We need to search the house."

"Use your phone to check the camera for the house and see if anyone's been by. I'll check the front gate. At least we'll know whether she's driven off the property."

Bailey gave a frantic nod and started to do as he'd suggested.

According to the app, no one had come in or gone out through the front gate since the last volunteer left over a half hour ago. "She's still here unless she's got another way out."

"No activity at the house either."

Paris's voice came over the speaker. "I'm heading your way now with Baker. Durant, stay at the store until we arrive. Walker and Bailey, I want you two to get back to the house and wait there until we have a game plan in place." With that, the call ended.

Jenny jogged out to her car and returned with a handheld radio that she tossed to Nate then held up five fingers to let him know what channel she'd be on. She gave Bailey a hug. "She's not going to get far. I'll keep you guys updated."

"Thank you." Bailey's voice shook as she returned the hug, reached for Nate's hand, and practically ran for the door. She didn't say another word as they drove to her house; she just leaned forward and scanned the area.

Back at the house, Minnie greeted them but then seemed to be searching for the boys.

Bailey walked from the front of the house to the back where she stared out the windows for several minutes before returning to the front. "I hate this. What if they're scared? What if she dropped them off somewhere, and they're out there wandering alone?" Her voice caught. "This is a nightmare."

Nate gently wrapped his arms around her and held her close. "We're going to find them." He said the words firmly, but inside, his confidence wavered.

For a moment, his mind went back to Lana's case. How many times had he reassured the little girl's mom that they were doing all they could to get her daughter back? He'd been in the room later when they had to deliver the worst news a parent can hear, and he'd never forgotten the mother's wails as she collapsed to the floor.

He prayed history wouldn't repeat itself.

"We're going to find them," he said again, this time with more conviction. "You hear me?"

She nodded against his chest. "I hear you."

"That means we need to be strong for them. We need clear heads so we can react quickly when news comes in or the situation shifts." He waited for her to raise her chin and look at him.

The remnants of tears were still there, but her jaw was set, and determination flashed in her eyes. Nate's respect for her soared.

He prayed aloud, asking God for wisdom and strength and for protection for the boys. "You might think waiting here is a waste of time because you want to go search for them. If they're out there on their own, this is where they'll come back to. They need you here when they do."

She nodded and took a step back as she used a sleeve to wipe away the tears. "I keep trying to figure out why she would've taken them. It makes no sense. If she was trying to make a fast getaway, they would only slow her down. There has to be a reason we don't know about yet."

The radio clipped to Nate's belt crackled. "It's Jenny. You guys there?"

"We're here."

"Logan ran phone records for both Rachel and Jeremy. They talk daily, sometimes several times a day. Officers arrived at Rachel's house. She isn't there, but they're going to stick around in case she comes back. Logan tried to ping her phone, but she must have powered it down. The same goes for Jeremy's."

"Have the police gone by Jeremy's house yet?"

The radio crackled again. "Yes, they just arrived on the scene. Jeremy isn't at home, but they are speaking to his wife. She had no idea that he'd gone by a different name before she met him. I get the impression there's a lot about him that she doesn't know."

Nate was beginning to believe Jeremy might have been responsible for Sophia's disappearance, but they still needed facts just like they needed to know why he was so intent on scaring Bailey into selling her place. He felt bad for Jeremy's wife and kids.

As though Bailey read his mind, she shook her head sadly. "I can't imagine being married to someone for years only to discover they weren't who you thought they were."

"Me, either. Even if Jeremy had nothing to do with Sophia's disappearance, there are obviously a lot of secrets that he's been keeping." He took her hand and pressed a kiss to the back. "I'd rather be told the truth, even if it's painful."

"Me, too."

Jenny's voice came over the radio. "Jeremy's car was seen parked on the shoulder of a country road that borders your land, Bailey. The car was empty. There's a good chance he's somewhere on your property or that he was meeting with Rachel. Stay alert."

Bailey walked over to a window and stared outside. Nate could barely make out some whispered words as she prayed, her hands braced against the doorframe.

Nate sent out his own silent plea.

"Nate!" Bailey's surprised cry had him crossing the room to her location. "It's Jordan!"

Chapter Thirty-Five

Bailey had been staring out the window and praying over her boys as well as the officers who were out there trying to find them. It seemed like forever ago that they, along with Nate, had hiked the little path that led away from her yard and into the trees behind it. She pictured her boys running beside each other, excited to see the barn, and fought against another round of tears that threatened to fall at any minute.

That's when she saw movement at the tree line. A moment later, Jordan's form ran into view as he raced down the path toward the house as fast as he could.

"Nate! It's Jordan!"

She immediately ran for the back door and flung it open, aware of Nate's footsteps right behind hers. When she reached Jordan, she went to her knees and gathered him close. She took in everything about him, from the smell of his hair to the way his little arms wrapped around her neck.

"Are you okay?" She shifted him away from her just enough to be able to look him over. She ran her hands down his arms. "Are you hurt?"

Nate placed a hand on the boy's shoulder and looked in the direction he'd come from. "Jordan, where's Seth?"

The poor boy's face was beet red as he sucked in air to catch his breath. Dirt mixed with tears had created muddy tracks down his cheeks. He pointed to the trees. "He told me to run."

Bailey's stomach clenched. "Who? Did Seth tell you to run?"

Jordan nodded. "Seth kicked the bad guy." He coughed and took in another breath. "Then told me to run home." His wide eyes filled with tears that shattered Bailey's heart.

Nate crouched down in front of him. "Was Miss Rachel the bad guy?"

With a shake of his head, Jordan pointed toward the trees again. "He got mad and tried to get Seth."

Bailey cradled her son's sweet face in her hands. "You're doing a great job, Jordan. Where is Seth? Do you know where he went?"

"The bad guy chased him. To the Hidden Barn." His chin quivered, and Bailey pulled him close again.

Nate reached down and helped her stand. "Take him in the house and lock all the doors. Stay inside." He gripped her arm and met her gaze, his own fierce with determination. "I'll find Seth."

All she could do was nod before he took off at a run, his gun in one hand and the radio in the other. "This is Nate. We have Jordan, but Seth is being pursued by a man near the old barn. I'm heading that way now, and I need backup..." His words faded as he disappeared into the brush.

"Come on, baby." Bailey scooped him into her arms and ran for the house. As soon as they were inside, she closed and locked the door, then made sure the same was true for the front.

Minnie started licking Jordan's arms and face as soon as Bailey set him down. The little boy wrapped his arms around the dog's neck.

"Honey, I'm going to get you a glass of water, and then I need you to tell me everything that happened."

●

Nate was thankful he'd gone for a walk on this path the other day because he knew exactly how to get to the old barn. He ran, his boots pounding the rock and dirt path until something above the trees caught his attention.

Smoke. It filled the sky. "Jenny, this is Nate. I'm seeing a lot of smoke ahead. The barn may be on fire. We're going to need support from the fire department ASAP."

"I'll make the call."

"I'm almost there. Going radio silent." Nate didn't wait for confirmation before he turned his radio off as he approached the bend in the path right before the old barn. Officers were on their way. With his gun drawn, he approached the barn cautiously. He needed to know where Seth was, and he had no idea whether Jeremy was armed or not.

He crouched behind a tree where he could see the barn. There were no visible flames, but smoke, dark and oppressive, billowed out and up. It probably didn't take much to get the old wood burning.

"Let me go!" Seth's voice came from the other side of the barn.

Nate ran in a crouch across the space between the tree line and the side of the barn closest to him. *Please, Lord, help me get to Seth in time. Keep him safe.* He proceeded down the length of the barn until he came to the corner.

There, he stepped out just enough to see what was going on.

A man gripped Seth by the upper arm and jerked him close, causing the boy to flinch. "Shut up, kid."

"You don't have to do this, Jer," Rachel pleaded. She was standing on Jeremy's other side, her arms outstretched. "Let Seth go. Give him to me. I'll make sure they let you go before I give him back."

Jeremy laughed, the sound forced and gravelly. "It's too late now. Do you really think the police would trade my freedom for this brat?" He shook Seth. "You promised they would never find out. You said I should trust you." He looked to his right at the burning building and laughed. "There's no way out of this now."

"Please, son. I did everything I could. Think of Rose and the girls. An accident in the past is one thing, but if you hurt Seth, you'll lose everything."

Nate gripped his gun, but there was no way to get a shot off without the risk of hitting Seth if things went wrong.

"I already have, thanks to you." He backhanded his mother, who stumbled and nearly fell. At the same time, Seth threw himself in the opposite direction, causing Jeremy to lose his grip on Seth's arm. Without hesitation, the boy sprinted toward the barn entrance. He skidded as he ran between the falling doors and disappeared inside.

Nate had to get him out of there before the fire caused it to collapse or Seth got himself lost inside.

Nate stepped forward. "Jeremy Price, put your hands in the air."

Jeremy started to raise his hands then reached over and jerked Rachel to her feet so she was between himself and Nate. "You're going to let me walk out of here."

Rachel's eyes went wide, a red welt beginning to form on her right cheek.

"You know I can't do that."

The sunlight caught on something behind Jeremy, and Nate noticed Paris and Baker approaching. No doubt there were other officers within sight. He kept his eyes trained on Jeremy.

"If you want to see that kid alive again, you will. He's probably baking in there already." Jeremy grinned as though the idea appealed to him. "You can take me on, or you can rescue the brat. The choice is yours."

Out of the corner of his eye, Nate saw Paris give a single nod. Nate re-holstered his weapon and held up his hands. "You're right, Jeremy. You're free to go. Just let me get to Seth. You don't want the murder of a little boy on your hands."

Jeremy sneered. "Good luck." He shoved Rachel away from him and turned to run.

Nate was barely aware of Paris shouting, "Destiny Police Department, put your hands in the air."

He ran to the barn and cautiously stepped between the doors. "Seth! Where are you?" He tried to see inside, but the darkness, plus the smoke, made it impossible. "Seth, it's Nate. We've got the bad guy. You can come out now."

"Help!" Coughing followed the faint cry.

Nate pulled the flashlight from his pocket and flipped it on. Smoke was everywhere, and he had no idea where Seth had gone. "God, please guide me to him." He took several more steps inside. "Seth! Where are you?"

"Nate. Help me!"

He turned in the direction of Seth's voice and found the boy sitting on the ground, his right foot caught in a broken floorboard.

"I can't get it out." He coughed, his eyes watering and tears flowing down his cheeks. "I don't want to stay here anymore."

"Hang in there, buddy. You and I are getting out of this together."

As Nate got closer, he dropped to his knees and then crawled to eliminate the possibility that he, too, might go through the floor. He gripped some of the wood that had trapped the boy's foot and yanked. It took three tries, but a satisfying crack sounded as the wood came free.

"Okay, let's see if we can get your foot out now." He helped Seth's foot through the hole.

Nate coughed as he grabbed the back of Seth's shirt to make sure he didn't lose the boy in the darkness. "Stay on your hands and knees. We're going to crawl out of here as fast as we can. Go!"

Together, they worked their way across the creaking floor toward where Nate knew the door was, even if he couldn't quite see it.

"Walker!"

"We're here." He yelled as loudly as he could. As soon as he saw the light streaming in from outside, he stood and scooped Seth into his arms, and ran the rest of the way.

They burst from the barn to find Paris waiting, relief on his face. "Thank God! You were about to make me play fire-fighter and come in there after you."

Nate started to laugh but ended up coughing instead. He turned his attention to Seth. "Are you okay?"

Seth coughed and laid his head against Nate's chest. "Did Jordan make it home?"

The boy's concern for his little brother over himself brought tears to Nate's eyes. "Yes, he's home with your mom. I'll bet they'll both be here soon. Are *you* okay?"

The boy nodded against Nate's chest. "I knew you'd find me."

Chapter Thirty-Six

I t took everything Bailey had to wait until Jenny stopped the car before flinging the back door open. She reached out for Jordan and together they ran to where Nate was holding Seth. Bailey threw her arms around them both and allowed the tears to flow freely. "Praise God, you're both okay." She picked up Jordan who put his arms around his big brother.

Bailey threaded a hand through the hair at the base of Nate's neck. "Thank you." She leaned in and pressed a short kiss to his lips before hugging all three of them closer.

The sounds of burning wood and crackling fire were punctuated by sirens as fire engines and an ambulance made their way into the clearing around the barn.

The next few minutes were a whirlwind as EMTs checked Nate and Seth for smoke inhalation and decided that they didn't need to be taken to the ER. Bailey sagged with relief. Things could've ended so differently. She refused to let her mind consider the possibilities.

Jenny came up and nudged Bailey's arm. "Rachel's asking to talk to you. She says she needs to tell you something because you'll understand. It's okay if you want to refuse."

Bailey's first instinct was to tell her no, but immediately afterward, she knew she would always wonder if she didn't talk to her. Nate looked over the boys' heads in concern.

"I'll speak with her, but I want Nate to come with me."

"Of course. You two go, and I'll stay with the boys." She knelt at their level. "We're going to watch the firefighters put out the fire, aren't we?"

They both nodded. Each of them took one of her hands.

Jenny looked up with tear-filled eyes. "She's in the back of Baker's car."

Nate put an arm around Bailey's shoulder and leaned in close. "You don't have to do this."

"I know." She leaned her head against his as they walked to Officer Baker's car. He gave them a nod and rolled a window down enough for them to see Rachel sitting in the back seat.

Rachel had clearly been crying, and she suddenly looked much older. She turned her body to face the door. "Bailey, I'm sorry. So sorry. I never intended for the boys to get hurt." Her voice cracked, and a sob escaped.

"But they were. They trusted you, Rachel, and so did I. Seth could've been killed in that barn."

Rachel shook her head. "I only wanted the police to let Jeremy go, and I was going to give the boys back. I promise I never would've harmed them. I didn't realize Jer..." Her voice trailed off, and she swallowed back a sob. "I was protecting my son. Surely you can understand that."

Bailey shook her head, words failing her. Of course, she'd do anything to protect her kids. But take someone else's and put them in harm's way? She'd like to think she'd never cross that line. "Did you know he murdered that girl?"

The older woman used her sleeve to wipe her eyes and nose. She nodded, unable to lift her gaze from the floor-board. "He said it was an accident. I chose to believe him, but I knew... He was so angry when she broke up with him. He wouldn't stop talking about her and how he was going to make her pay for leaving him." She raised her chin then, and regret shone in her eyes. "He buried her under the floorboards in the storage room of the barn."

Bailey fought back the nausea that bubbled up in her stomach. It was bad enough that Jeremy murdered that girl, but Rachel had helped him cover it up all these years. Officer Baker, who was standing nearby, exchanged a look with Nate and moved away.

Bailey's eyes narrowed. "That's why you wanted the job working for me."

Rachel nodded and had the good sense to look ashamed of herself. "I thought I could keep an eye on the place. Jeremy had gotten married and started a family. He'd turned his life around. All I needed was for the truth to stay hidden, and he could have the normal life he deserved."

It was all Bailey could do to not scream at the woman. The normal life he deserved? What about Sophia? Her life had been stolen from her.

Rachel continued to talk. "I kept hoping you'd sell the place, and then I could buy it, and I'd never have to worry about it again. And then the watch turned up, and you started talking about having the barn demolished." She hung her head again. "When I told Jeremy, he got angry. He told me that since I hadn't taken care of things, he was going to have to do it."

Take care of it how? Make things so horrible that Bailey was forced to leave? Or had he intended on eventually killing her? Everything would've gone to Seth and Jordan, and no doubt the farm would've been sold and the money kept in a trust for the boys. If it'd gotten that far, Jeremy just might have gotten what he wanted. The sad thing was, Rachel still probably didn't believe he was capable of such a thing.

She shivered, and Nate placed a protective hand on her back. With a glance at him, she shook her head. That was about all she had in her when it came to Rachel. She wanted to get back to her boys.

Bailey started to turn away when Rachel called out to her.

"Don't act so high and mighty. You would've done the same thing." She raised her voice. *"The same thing!"*

●

Bailey accepted the hot chocolate and noted the four marshmallows floating on top. She glanced at Nate over the rim of the mug and smiled. "I feel spoiled. Thank you."

Nate kissed the top of her head and took a seat across the table from her, his own mug in his hands. "Are you kidding? After the day you've had, you deserve to be pampered." With a flourish, he pulled a package of Reese's Peanut Butter Cups from the front pocket of his denim jacket and handed them to her. "This seemed like a double chocolate kind of night."

"You, sir, are not wrong." She opened the package and handed one to him. "I'm just glad the boys went to sleep okay. I wasn't sure if they'd be able to after everything." They were probably too exhausted to fight it tonight. She suspected nightmares would come, though, and prayed she was wrong.

Minnie wandered over and rested her chin on Nate's knee.

Nate ran a hand over her head. "Sorry, girl, no chocolate for you."

"You know, you don't have to stay here tonight. You and Minnie could go home. Sleep in an actual bed. You've got to be tired of the couch."

He shrugged. "We'll need to go back tomorrow, but I'm not in a hurry tonight." When he looked at her, there was no missing the worry in his eyes. "I don't want to leave you and the boys alone after everything you've been through today."

She reached across the table for his hand. "I appreciate that." The candy tasted amazing, and it was even better when she washed it down with a sip of her hot chocolate. "You went through a lot today, too. It's probably better for you to be around people."

"Yeah, it is." He set his mug down and gave her hand a squeeze. "When I was running down that path to find Seth, I was so worried I wouldn't be able to get to him in time."

"You were thinking about Lana."

He gave a short nod.

"But you did find him, Nate. And you got to him in time. Thanks to you, my son is asleep upstairs in his own bed." Bailey's voice broke. "I can only imagine how horrible that case must have been. It would permanently scar anyone. But you were an amazing police officer. Joe could never say enough good things about you. If you ever decide to go back, this town and everyone in it will be better because of it. Because of you."

Epilogue
Three Weeks Later

Nate waved goodbye to Tia at the front desk of the Destiny Police Department and jogged out of the building to his truck. He couldn't wait to see Bailey and the boys. The last few weeks had been crazy busy since he'd decided to accept Chief Dolman's offer to get his job back. It wasn't an easy process. There were tests to take, evaluations to go through, and enough paperwork to make his head swim.

He punched in the code to get onto the Thompson Family Farms and drove past the store. After everything that happened, Bailey chose to close the farm to the public for the time being. Not only did she not have enough help to run the store, but she was worried there'd be too much interest from the public when it came to the barn and the murder of Sophia Tinsley.

While he hated to see her give it up, he agreed completely that it was the wisest course of action for now. Thankfully, once the news had run the story, things calmed down a little, and people had mostly left Bailey alone.

He found her and the boys at the goat pen. Jordan and

Seth were standing on one of the fence rails and feeding the goats pieces of lettuce and carrots. Bailey was watching from nearby with Minnie.

Bailey turned and flashed him a brilliant smile. Her beautiful dark blonde hair flowed around her shoulders, and those gray-blue eyes sparkled. Man, this was seriously his favorite part of the day.

He'd barely stepped out of his truck when both boys ran over to give him a hug. Jordan lifted a large lettuce leaf. "Do you wanna feed the goats, too?"

"Maybe in a few minutes, buddy. I'm going to talk to your mom first, okay?"

"Okay!" With that, the boys got back to sharing their produce with the goats.

Minnie tried to run toward him, her whole body wriggling with excitement. As soon as Bailey let the leash go, the dog flew into Nate's legs with a happy whine. He laughed as he petted her and picked up her leash.

Finally, he strode to where Bailey was waiting and pulled her into his arms before kissing her thoroughly. When he ended the kiss, he placed another right on that cute little dimple of hers. "I'm really glad to see you," he said, his voice just above a whisper.

"I'm glad to see you, too." She stood on her tiptoes for another kiss. "How was your day?" Her brows furrowed in concern.

He kissed her there and then laced his fingers with hers. "It was rough, but I'm glad I went."

Paris had invited him to make the trip back to Austin to return Sophia's watch to her father. It'd taken a while to get it released from evidence. The fire department was able to put the fire out before the entire old barn went up in flames, but it was several days before anyone could get in to investigate further.

The police finally went in through the side wall and found the remains of Sophia right where Rachel said they would be. Once everything was finalized with the case, the remains would be returned to Mr. Tinsley.

"He broke down when he saw the watch, but I think we were finally able to give him some closure. He'll finally be able to lay his daughter to rest. I'm just praying he'll find some peace now."

"I've been praying for him, too."

Nate raised her hand and kissed her thumb. "How about a walk by the sunflowers? They'll only be around for another week or two, right?"

"If that." She turned and addressed the boys. "Come on, guys. Let's go for a walk. Then we'll go home and eat dinner."

The boys found sticks and ran a little ahead of the adults, dragging the sticks behind them to make trails in the dirt. Nate let Minnie off her leash so she could trot along with them. It only took a few minutes to reach the sunflower field. The sun was dropping low in the sky, and the golden light painted an amazing picture behind the sea of flowers.

While the boys played, Nate stood behind Bailey and curled an arm around her waist.

"I think I've made a decision about this place." Bailey glanced back at him.

"Oh?" Nate knew she'd been struggling with whether she wanted to continue living on the farm or if selling it might be the better option. He'd told her he supported whatever she wanted to do, and he still felt that way.

"I'd like to keep about ten acres of it and sell the rest. I really love it out here, and I like the idea of having some land so we can keep the goats, have a big garden, or do anything else we want to do. But the farm and everything else is a lot." She leaned back against his chest.

"I think that sounds like a great plan. Are you thinking about having a new house built?"

"Maybe. It seems like a big decision to make on my own." She tipped her head back just enough to look at him, and a mischievous smile curled her lips.

They hadn't talked about marriage outright, but they'd both danced around the subject enough to know it was on the horizon.

"I couldn't agree more. Then we'll just have to figure it out together, won't we?" He kissed the tip of her nose.

"I like the sound of that." Her voice sounded wistful.

"So do I." He moved to stand in front of her, reached into his pocket, and pulled out the ring that he'd chosen a week ago. It wasn't huge or fancy, but the moment he saw it, he knew it was made for Bailey. He got down on one knee and held it out in front of him. "Bailey, I realize all of this is still kind of new between us, but I've loved you for as long as I've known you. You're my best friend, and I want to go through life with you by my side." He took in a steadying breath and memorized the way her eyes sparkled and that little smile played at the corners of her mouth. "Will you marry me?"

"Without hesitation. I love you, Nate."

"I love *you*." He stood, slipped the ring onto her finger, and pulled her close for a kiss that left them both breathless. "Hey, check it out." Nate gently turned her in his arms so she was facing the sunset behind the field of flowers.

"Absolutely breathtaking."

"Yes, you are." He put his arms around her waist and

nuzzled her neck. "No matter which ten acres we choose to keep, we have to have a sunflower field."

"Agreed." She looked down at her left hand. "This ring is perfect."

Seth and Jordan ran over to them with Minnie on their heels, their sticks forgotten.

"I'm starving." Jordan patted his belly.

"Can we go home? I'm ready for some pizza." Seth asked. He looked up at Nate. "Are you eating with us tonight?"

Nate ruffled the boy's hair. "Are you kidding? I wouldn't miss it for the world."

Special Thanks

Doug and Sydney, I want to send a special thanks to you both. I had a pretty tight deadline with this book, and the two of you did all you could to make sure I had enough time to write. Seriously, this book wouldn't be here otherwise. I love you guys!

Elizabeth and Melissa, thank you for all of your encouragement and for cheering me on this time around. It made such a huge difference, especially after some of those late nights.

Many thanks to my sweet early readers. Steph and Denny, you ladies are always awesome at catching those typos that slip through. More than anything else, your friendships are such a blessing.

Have I mentioned how amazing my ARC team is? I'm so thankful for each and every one of you!

Last but not least, I praise You, Father God, for Your unending love and blessings. Your love truly never fails.

About the Author

Melanie D. Snitker is a *USA Today* bestselling author who writes inspirational romance and romantic suspense. She and her husband live in Texas with their two children. They share their home with two dogs and two terrariums filled with small critters. In her spare time, Melanie enjoys photography, reading, training her dog, playing computer games, and hanging out with family and friends.

https://www.melaniedsnitker.com/
https://www.facebook.com/melaniedsnitker
https://www.instagram.com/
https://x.com/MelanieDSnitker
https://www.bookbub.com/authors/melanie-d-snitker
http://www.goodreads.com/melaniedsnitker

Books by Melanie D. Snitker

Danger in Destiny

Out of the Ashes

Frozen in Jeopardy

Beneath the Surface

Caught in the Crosshairs

Running from the Past

In Search of the Truth

Assigned to Protect

Brides of Clearwater

Marrying Mandy

Marrying Raven

Marrying Chrissy

Marrying Bonnie

Marrying Emma

Marrying Noel

Books by Melanie D. Snitker

Love's Compass Complete Series

Finding Peace

Finding Hope

Finding Courage

Finding Faith

Finding Joy

Finding Grace

Love Unexpected Complete Series

Safe In His Arms

Someone to Trust

Starting Anew

Healing Hearts

Calming the Storm

I Still Do

Don't Kiss Me Goodbye

Sage Valley Ranch

Charmed by the Daring Cowboy

Welcome to Romance

Fall Into Romance

A Merry Miracle in Romance